THE
BLACK
CATHEDRAL

THE
BLACK
CATHEDRAL

MARCIAL GALA

Translated from the Spanish by
ANNA KUSHNER

FARRAR, STRAUS AND GIROUX

NEW YORK

Farrar, Straus and Giroux
120 Broadway, New York 10271

Library of Congress Cataloging-in-Publication Data
Names: Gala, Marcial, 1963– author. | Kushner, Anna, translator.
Title: The Black cathedral / Marcial Gala ; translated from the
   Spanish by Anna Kushner.
Other titles: Catedral de los negros. English
Description: First American edition. | New York : Farrar, Straus and
   Giroux, 2020. | Originally published in Spanish in 2012 by
   Letras Cubanas, Cuba, as La catedral de los negros.
Identifiers: LCCN 2019037907 | ISBN 9780374118013 (hardcover)
Subjects: LCSH: Cuba—Fiction.
Classification: LCC PQ7390.G24 C3813 2020 | DDC 863/.64—dc23
LC record available at https://lccn.loc.gov/2019037907

Designed by Gretchen Achilles

Our books may be purchased in bulk for promotional, educational,
or business use. Please contact your local bookseller or the
Macmillan Corporate and Premium Sales Department at
1-800-221-7945, extension 5442, or by e-mail at
MacmillanSpecialMarkets@macmillan.com.

www.fsgbooks.com
www.twitter.com/fsgbooks • www.facebook.com/fsgbooks

1   3   5   7   9   10   8   6   4   2

Endpaper illustration by Thomas Colligan

Cuba has its cathedrals in the future.

—JOSÉ LEZAMA LIMA

PART

ONE

MARIBEL GARCÍA MEDINA

Besides David King and Samuel Prince, there was an older one, Mary Johannes, she was called, or still is, because she's alive and things are going better for her than for us. They arrived in Punta Gotica one day in an old Ford truck with Camagüey plates. I remember them unloading their stuff. *Too much furniture for someone moving into a neighborhood like this*, I thought from the first.

YOHANDRIS CARLOS FERNÁNDEZ RAMÍREZ, *a.k.a.* GUTS

I was playing soccer when they arrived. *This can't be good*, I thought, because the girl riding in the truck's cab was fanning herself and looking at the neighborhood as if they'd dropped her right at the doors to hell. "One more sucker in town," I said out loud, and went back to doing my thing. The guys were just kids then; Cricket, the older one, already looked like a total nutjob. *I can take that one, I'll hack him down like a palm tree*, I thought, because he was very tall. "Guts, he's so tall he can't scratch his own ass," Nacho Fat-Lips said, and passed me the ball.

MARIBEL

I've lived here for years, but that doesn't mean I'm tied down here. The thing is that this place, before the riffraff began moving in, was a rooming house for sailors. That was back in the time of the other government, and a nephew of President Machado himself lived in one of the rooms. He'd also met José Martí's son, you know, that Ismaelillo—and actually, it seems that Martí wasn't as famous then as he is now, when he shows up all over the place and you can't even turn on the TV without hearing, "As the apostle of Cuban independence said," and, well, it gets a little old. They say that Ismaelillo was in the business of renting out rooms, and one of his customers was this nephew of Machado's, who owed him for about six months. He didn't charge him because, on the day that he personally went to kick him out of the house, all of Martí's works were there in a bookcase, cared for like they were made of gold, and Ismaelillo got sentimental and forgave Machado's relative, who, now that I think of it, must have been his nephew by marriage, because no matter how cheap he was, a former president wouldn't have his sister's son renting one of these little rooms that get miserable as hell on a hot day, now would he? But back to the folks from Camagüey: when they got here, it had been three months since I'd broken up with Chago, and, well, I really had a thing for everything from the eastern part of the island, and when I heard they were from around there, I went to take a look at the move, specifically so that I could drop a few snide comments here and there to see if the new neighbor had it in her to hop over and say something to me, to show me up front what this family was really made of.

BERTA

I didn't see them arrive, since I was at school. It was my mother who told me that old Castillo's place had been taken over by a family with a girl who was more or less my age, but that she didn't want us getting together right away. "First you have to get to know people," she said. "That's why things happen to you, you're too trusting." I told her it was fine, that I didn't really want to meet anyone anyway, but after I changed out of my uniform, since I didn't have anything else to do, I sat at the door to our house and looked over at the place that used to belong to Castillo, an old man who, as mean-spirited gossip had it, died of cirrhosis.

MARIBEL

All of it could have been avoided if they hadn't drawn so much attention, but ever since they arrived, with their stuck-up faces and wearing that fancy gear, the people in the neighborhood fell all over themselves for them. "Did you meet the folks from Camagüey?" Lucy the gum seller asked me, taking over a little plate of sweet potato pudding to the girl, who, according to the mother, was in delicate health. I had seen that young girl and she seemed healthy as a horse, thin, with slanted eyes, a beautiful black girl, yes, but full of herself—now she lives in Italy, all the ones like her end up over there.

That man from Camagüey ate, lived, and breathed Jesus Christ, always had Him at the tip of his tongue. The day of their arrival, he threw five pesos at the kids who were playing soccer so they would help him unload the stuff, and then he came over to greet us. He had a polite smile and a thin, strong, dry hand. "Blessings," he said. "My name is Arturo and this is my wife, Carmen." "Blessings," echoed that Carmen, who was walking a few steps behind; you could tell she was too hot for

5

a guy like him, in his fifties and pretty run-down, you could tell that wouldn't end well. I was shocked when he introduced the kids, since they didn't seem like they were hers. The three of them were tall, especially the older boy, David, he was a real beanpole and only thirteen years old. The younger one, Prince, held out his elegant, slightly sweaty hand and looked at us with those same slanted eyes as his mother and his sister, and I thought, *This one's a fairy.*

"Please, can you tell me where the Church of the Holy Sacrament is?" the guy asked.

"Church of the Holy Sacrament?" was the response. "There's never been anything like that here."

GUTS

Jelly, Barbarito, Lupe's kid, named him, as soon as he saw him reading right in the middle of the day, as if there were no soccer to play, no girls to check out, no kite to fly, no gas to pass. He said to me, "Guts, if this guy isn't a fairy, he knows where the pixie dust is," especially since the kid was wearing some tight pants, a little too short, that were ugly as sin. "That's the fashion in Camagüey," Berta had to say, she was already defending him back then, saying he looked like Michael Jackson before he bleached his skin, that he was a beautiful black boy like none other in the neighborhood and that he was good enough to eat; "not like his brother, who you can tell is kind of loony."

"That one's queerer than a three-dollar bill," Barbarito insisted. "You'll see."

The truth is that we were innocent back then, even if our future was already wasted. NO ONE GETS OUT OF THIS NEIGHBORHOOD ALIVE, someone had written on the side of a house, because the neighborhood was bad, really and truly bad. If you're born black, you're already screwed; imagine if, in addition, you have to live in the squalid rooming houses of a neighborhood like this; and I'm a university graduate, a psychologist, and even have a master's in business administration, you'd think I wouldn't be so fucked. But with a salary of four hundred pesos and no bonus in foreign currency, what can you possibly come up with? Nothing—Armageddon. I didn't see them arrive; they called me when the younger one, Prince, split open Lupe's kid Bárbaro's head. He did it with a book, terrible, blood everywhere, and I said, "Somebody's going to get it," because that Lupe isn't rational, she's a fat black woman with arms that look like Muhammad Ali's and a temper that, well, I don't know what to compare it to, but to say it's short would be an understatement. "Does his mother know yet?" I asked, while I cleaned up the kid's wound.

"Not yet, she's out, busting her ass."

"When she finds out, she's gonna make a lot of noise."

"That Jelly is going to pay for this, I'll make him suck my balls, goddammit, I'll cut off his dick, shit, goddamn," Barbarito said, his eyes tearing up, not looking like he could hurt anyone.

Jelly: because he was like a dark substance almost like water, but when you look closer, you realize it's fat, thick, and heavy; Jelly, because he looked at us with those wide eyes like a girl's, he was really thin, he'd smile at the drop of a hat, and then get into some terrible fights. He knew how to fight, not with his hands, but by picking up rocks, sand, sticks, cans, whatever there was. He hit Barbarito with the edge of a book; it was a quick, skilled, and cunning blow, as if he'd practiced a lot. *This dude has a future in the neighborhood*, I thought, *if Lupe doesn't throw the whole family out on their ass, she'll make such a racket that they'll pack up and fly back to Camagüey, they won't know how to react when Lupe comes around asking about her son's cracked skull and stands there with her feet planted, screaming for someone to take responsibility, with a "Go to hell" and a "Fuck your mother" to everyone from Camagüey, Ciego de Ávila, the eastern part of the island, and even from Haiti.*

AURORA, *neighbor*

They had been in Cienfuegos for three days and had already cracked somebody's skull, and not just anyone's: it was Bárbaro, Lupe's son, Urbieta's stepson. That day, the parents and the girl, that Johannes, who always rubbed me the wrong way, had gone out. At home, only the two boys were left, so the younger one, after Bárbaro came out screaming and bleeding, he went inside as if nothing had happened and I think he started watching television. He didn't say, "I'll kill anyone who calls me a *maricón*," he didn't say, "I'm a *maricón* but whoever calls me that has to fuck me or I'll kill him," he didn't say, "You've got to jerk me off," he didn't say, "You have no respect," none of that; all he did, when Bárbaro approached him and said to him, "You're like a little bit of jelly that I just want to eat up, you're hotter than your sister, and, man, she's hot," he picked up his book, turned it on its side, and dropped it, with shocking speed, and that was the end of Barbarito being fresh, that was as far as he got.

MARIBEL

I mean, what kind of black person thinks of naming their sons David King and Samuel Prince, that's just setting them up to think they deserve the world. I would have named one of them Nardo and the other one Paco and that would be that, and if they didn't like it, they could deal with it; although now that I think about it, any name can fuck you up or get you fucked.

The book was one of those that has a hard cover, although it wasn't a Bible, or something by Lenin, or a volume of Martí's complete works, it was some kind of poetry, I'm sure of it because it had a lot of little figures on the front and didn't seem like it would be about anything too serious, but anyway, he really clocked Bárbaro with that book. *If that didn't teach him his letters, they're never getting in there*, I thought. You have to be really tough to hit someone like that when you've just moved in, really tough or really ignorant of how things work in a neighborhood like this one, you have to be from Pinar del Río, actually, and not from Camagüey.

Hit him, give him a hard one to the belly, then take him to the train tracks and crush his head against the rails and wait for a train to come, then force him to put a foot on the line, if he's left-handed, then the left one, if he's right-handed, then the other one, then piss on him, first once, then again, piss on him, and if you still feel like it, shit on his face, but don't let him touch your ass while you're shitting on him, you don't want anyone to think you're a fag, do him in, he's not worth a dime, finish him, so you get respect and not whatever the hell it is they think of you now. That's what my mother told me when Jelly cracked my skull, she said, *Let's go, dammit, we're going so you can crack his skull open, I'll fuck up anyone who gets in the way.*

"Let's go."

GUTS

When they came over, a cowboy show was on TV, not like the crap shows they have today, but the old ones, the ones with the Villalobos brothers, and all of us kids were focused on the TV. Anyway, three knocks came at the door, sounding like cannon fire.

BÁRBARO

That Arturo opened the door for us.

"Blessings. How can I help you good people?" he said to us, in that way he had of speaking, so soft it was like he had a turd stuck in his throat.

"I don't even believe in my own mother who birthed me, so save your breath," my mother said. "Your good-for-nothing son cracked open Barbarito's head and he has to come out and fight him. Barbarito is nobody's fool, he needs to be shown some respect. So let's have your little gumdrop, or whatever the fuck he is. I don't understand a thing, you're going to have hell to pay."

I don't understand a thing, you're going to have hell to pay. That was how my mother talked. Later, after she had the stroke, Urbieta, who had already gotten out of jail, left her for someone else, and my mother, fifty-some years old, had to spend her days washing floors, white people's floors, and since the stroke had left her kind of dopey, no one respected her. *La Lupe, your son is a transvestite*, they would say to her, *a* maricón.

"Swear it isn't true," she would say to me when she saw me come in.

"Of course it's not true," I would assure her. "I'm a man. It's art, what I do, I get dressed and make myself up as a woman as a form of art."

"It was Jelly who got that into your head, who hurt you, that son of a bitch. You were so macho, my son, very macho. You never liked *pinga*, I know you didn't."

"No, *mamá*," I'd say, and as I closed my eyes, it would be that April afternoon again, when my mother and I went to the Stuarts' house to bust Jelly's head.

"David King, present yourself," Stuart said.

So Cricket popped out his crazy-ass face.

"Not that one," I said. "It was the other one."

"What do you mean, the other one?" the father said. "Take a good look at him, boy, surely it was this one."

"No," I said. "It was the other one, the gentle one."

"Impossible. The other one is an irreproachable gentleman."

"Irreproachable, my ass," said my mother. "Call him out here before I come in and find him."

"Go in, David King," the man said, and then, "Listen, ma'am, why don't we straighten all this out inside the house. I'm sure that with God's favor, we can come to an agreement."

"No," my mother said. "Tell that worthless son of yours to come out already. If you don't, I'll be the one who goes in there and starts swinging."

"Excuse me, but you will not go into my house without my permission, and I assure you that your son must be mistaken. Samuel Prince is incapable of treating another of God's children like that . . . Come in the right way and let's settle this. At the end of the day, we're not animals, the spirit of God dwells within us all."

"Speak for yourself."

"Come in," the man insisted. "Please."

MARIBEL

A guy who used money to settle things, like the white people in Punta Gorda—he had that defect, or that virtue, depending on how you look at it. He paid la Lupe five hundred pesos to keep her quiet, at least that's what she said, maybe she settled for fifty; la Lupe, tough act and all, she was always a pushover. You would've had to kill me—I'll smash the brains out of anyone who touches a child of mine. "The guy's a real moneybags," the whole neighborhood said, and people began to beat down his door; if someone stole a bicycle, they went to see him: *Arturo, you dig these wheels? See how new this is, it's straight from the store.* If a woman was trying to hustle, she would wait for Carmen to leave before going to see him: *Listen, Arturo, I need a hundred pesos and don't have any way to pay you back . . . Look, here's my body.* But he was all "Blessings, sister," he said the same thing to everyone, without getting into any business; and as for the whores, they soon stopped visiting him. It was around then that the bigger of the two boys decided to start singing; that's when we named him Cricket, because what came out of his mouth was pure honey, he coulda been in a reggaeton band, that voice of his was so good.

GUTS

We let Cricket in from the beginning. He was kind of crazy, but at least he didn't seem like a fairy and he played soccer pretty good. But his thing was baseball. When we said to him, *Hey, man, we don't play ball here, you've got to get outta the neighborhood for that,* he was kind of sad, but then he forgot about it. I was sure he was kind of slow, like my brother Tere, who was at Tato Madruga, the school for retards, and I'd ask him things: "Hey, Cricket, how much is six times six?"

"Thirty-six," he would say, and I would tell myself, *It can't be thirty-six, this idiot doesn't know,* but when I asked other people, they also said it had been thirty-six for years and should still be, unless math had changed and the news hadn't reached the neighborhood yet.

Later, I'd ask him, "Hey, Cricket, what's the deal with America? Who discovered it?"

"Columbus."

"So was Columbus white or black?"

"White, Guts, blond and blue-eyed."

Basically, he knew a lot for a brown kid, 'cause that's what he was, brown, but I liked him; it was the other one I couldn't stand, he was too pretty, always so clean, always reading. His parents treated him even more gently than the girl, who really was hot.

MARIBEL

He hated for his son to sing. If he came home early from work and heard Cricket's voice, he'd say to everyone, "Blessings," and then he'd say, "One artist in the family is enough. Come in, David King," and the kid would go into the house without daring to lift his head to look at his father. We soon found out that he beat him, Guts was the one who said so; he went up on the roof, peeked in a window, and saw how old Stuart removed his wide leather belt to hit his son on the back. After that, we thought Cricket wouldn't sing anymore, but with that kid, singing was an obsession. As soon as old Stuart went out to the shop with his mechanic's tools, Cricket would start singing. It didn't matter to him if it was a Marco Antonio Solís song or a bolero by Orlando Contreras, it didn't matter if Aurora, Berta's mom, took out her guitar to accompany him or if Nacho Fat-Lips started to play a rumba on the box drum, and when there was no accompaniment, he did it a cappella, Cricket sang whatever. His mother would come to the door and say, *David, please, stop that, your father will lose it with me.*

The Church of the Holy Sacrament of the Resurrected
Christ . . . When Stuart arrived from Camagüey, no more than
a dozen people in Cienfuegos had heard of our congregation,
and across the whole province, there weren't even twenty of
us, eight of whom lived in Aguada and three in Cruces, making
it difficult to depend on them for anything practical. The
pastor of the Cienfuegos Sacramentalists was named Basulto,
an intelligent young guy, but cold and aloof. Arturo Stuart
had charisma and a knack with crowds, he was a natural leader,
and a church like the Sacramentalist one, which is inspired by
ancient Greek rites, fit like a glove on someone given to manners and mystery. Besides, he had his son Prince. The kid knew
how to speak. He knew how to be convincing. He had read the
Bible with purpose and knew how to cite verses correctly. Even
his siblings would fall silent, watching him as if the angel of
the Lord himself were speaking through his mouth. Everybody
liked that; Cubans have a penchant for the corny and sentimental, and on worship Sundays, Basulto's house would fill up.
Certainly another factor was that Arturo had cemented friend-
ships with the denomination's pastors in several U.S. states,
and they began to send us contributions, or assistance, as we
also called it. Such assistance took the form of electric razors,
soap, toys for the children, shoes, clothing, and kitchen uten-
sils, even Bibles, worship books and videos, which gave us an
idea of the Sacramentalist church's power in the U.S. In six
months, we went from twenty people to almost a thousand;
few, in a sense, but for a congregation as strict as the Sacramentalists', that was legion. So, Basulto's house, big as it was, came

to be completely insufficient, and we decided to worship at the house of our good sister Elizabet.

RICARDO MORA GUTIÉRREZ, *a.k.a.* GRINGO

I had killed my first guy. I slashed his neck and didn't stop until his eyes were like a dead cow's. "Who has the biggest cock now?" I asked him, then I cleaned the switchblade with the sleeveless shirt he had been wearing to show off.

"Now what do we do, Gringo?" Pork Chop asked me.

"That's the easy part. We cut him up—the guy came from Cabaiguán, no one is going to miss him. You'll see. Get the bike, but pedal slowly, you don't want anyone to mess with you, and start telling suckers that you have some high-quality meat. When you're done with that, go to the hiding place and bring over the boning knife. But first, wash yourself and change your clothes, 'cause you fucking reek of moonshine."

"But we don't have any," Pork Chop said.

"But we don't have any what? Soap?"

"Meat, Gringo, meat."

"What about this? Grade A meat."

"Damn, Gringo, you're a genius."

"You ain't seen nothin' yet . . . Get moving, but calmly. I'll start preparing this veal."

He came all the way from Santiespíritu to end up like this, some guys really are a special kind of stupid, I thought, looking at the deceased, who had been left with an idiotic expression on his face that made me feel a smidgen of pity, but, "You gotta fuck life before it fucks you," my mother used to say, and this guy had come to fuck us, so he got what he had coming to him.

The first thing I did was remove his huge-ass gold chain, then I took out the wad of cash from his backpack and found the piece, one of those Makarovs that always jams. *What a useless piece of shit you are*, I thought. *Who thinks of putting a gun in his backpack? Idiots must be a dime a dozen in Cabaiguán.*

"Hey, man, do you know where you can buy a motorcycle, a really good one, an MZT or something like that, none of this Carpati or Benjovina shit?" the guy had asked me right at the door of La Mimbre. I was selling shades, but the minute I saw him, I thought this *guajiro*, this peasant, had cash.

"I might know," I told him. "Who can say, the only fortune-teller here is God."

"But it has to have the paperwork in order. I came from Cabaiguán because they had one set aside for me, and when I got here, they didn't have the title."

"This one has everything. It's just waiting for a guy like you to ride it . . . It's almost new."

"I like that. Is it an MZT?"

"No, a Harley-Davidson that my cousin the sailor brought from Panama."

"Really?"

"Just like I said."

"It's going to be really expensive."

"No, about the same as a Jawa, and it's got the kind of engine that, well, when you ride it into Cabaiguán, all of those *guajiros* are going to go nuts."

"Let's go see it."

17

"Do you have the money on you?"

The useless piece of shit said yes, then he saw something in my eyes, regretted it, and said he had hidden it at the house of a girlfriend just in case.

I said, "You're not a cop, are you?"

"Cop? Me? No way, I'm a normal guy."

"You can tell, but we're already talking too much. Let's go to my cousin's house so you can see the hog."

"Let's go." I took him to San Lázaro, and he was all, "Your cousin lives in a pretty bad place."

"The thing is, his wife threw him out and he had to come here, motorcycle and all, and he's scared about it getting stolen, that's why he's going to sell it, for peace of mind."

We got to Pork Chop's room:

"Cuz? Listen, *tarugo*, are you there?"

"What a surprise, Gringo, how's life going, my man?" Piggy said from inside with a grin ear to ear, thinking I had come to collect the money he owed me, but you could tell that he'd been drinking, he stank of rotgut and piss and the *guajiro* practically took off.

"I'll wait for you outside."

"These sailors really drink a lot." I smiled. "But have a seat, man, have a seat."

The *guajiro* sat down, and I asked Piggy, "Hey, *tarugo*, how's the bike?"

What bike? he was going to ask, but I winked at him.

"Oh, yeah, the bike. It's around. I lent it out."

"You lent it out? That's not the kind of thing you lend out. To who?"

"Mariana's guy."

18

"Oh, well, I don't have any problem with him . . . When's he bringing it back? Our friend here is interested in the hog."

"In a little while; he needed it to go to Varadero."

"On a machine like that you can go to Varadero in minutes, it runs faster than a Ferrari."

"Runs? It flies. Especially since I have it in tip-top shape, it doesn't need anything."

"Besides, the Harley is a classic, the best there is in motorcycles."

"You said it."

"Look, here, go get six beers over there, but get Bucaneros." I made as if to put my hand in my pocket, but the *guajiro* was faster.

"Forget it." He opened his backpack and took out his wad of cash, and that was his mistake; he thought he was so young and strong with that bull's neck and those big mitts, he waltzed into the lion's den for a beer. What a moron, it still surprises me. I had to wait for him to drink three Bucanero beers and then say, "I'm going to the bathroom," and while Pork Chop talked to him, I got behind him, took out my switchblade, and quickly slit his throat so he wouldn't scream.

When Pork Chop came back, I had already counted the money and I had the guy naked on top of the sink. "Did you bring everything?"

Pork Chop opened the bag and showed me the hammer, the knives, and a machete.

"Did you tell the chumps we had steak?"

"Yes, of course."

"Who'd you talk to?"

"The ones in Punta Gorda. Those *blancos* are going to be eating dead person for a week."

"They deserve it. Let's get started." I grabbed the boning knife.

"You're really something, Gringo."

"What I am is a guy with money." I showed Pork Chop the big wad of bills. "Do you know how many are here? A thousand bills of a hundred each."

"And how much is that?"

"How much do you think?"

"I don't know, you tell me."

"You're such an idiot, Piggy, such an idiot."

"Lucky you that you're smart."

"Well, now we'll see if that little black girl from Camagüey gives me a chance, we'll see."

GUTS

Gringo liked her as soon as he saw her. *A black girl for taking out on the town, she has Beyoncé's body and the face of an angel, and she's going to be mine*, he said, and it was as if he had branded her, no one in the neighborhood would dare mess with her.

"Pass it to me, *loco*, pass it to me!" I was shouting to Cricket, because that was his problem, he thought he was Messi, he didn't give the ball to anyone. Plenty of times I wanted to fight him after we lost a match because he thought he could handle everything like he was Ronaldinho Gaúcho himself. I'd get right on him, *Next time you pass it or I'll fuck you up!* That was before we knew that Gringo was all gaga over the sister and that it was dangerous to threaten to hit Cricket, because

Gringo was a super inconvenient guy to cross, he was a Palo initiate, and besides, he seemed to be suddenly flush with cash; he showed up in the neighborhood one day riding a bike from the shopping center, he rang the bell and shouted, "I demand respect!" And everyone knew that Gringo was loaded, more so when he invited the whole neighborhood to drink beer, not just crappy little cans, or even bottles, but an enormous keg on wheels. Good old lager, and lots of it, but anyway, the keg stopped, attached to a tractor and everything, in front of one of the entrances to the neighborhood, and each family got a tub apiece. By ten at night, everyone was drunk, even the kids. It was pure pandemonium. All the families drank, except for the one from Camagüey, because when Gringo showed up at the Stuarts' door with eight cans of Bucanero beer and two cola drinks, the old man practically kicked him out.

GRINGO

"Hey," I said to him.

"Blessings," he said. "What do you desire?"

"I'm sharing, my friend, sharing," I began, which was my first mistake because the old man didn't like being called that.

"I'm not your friend."

"Yes, I know, it's a figure of speech. How would you like me to address you? *Compañero?* Fine then, no problem; I'll call you *compañero* and that's that."

"Oxen are *compañeros*. It's better to call me Mr. Stuart, or if that bothers you, Arturo Stuart or just Arturo."

"Whatever you say . . . Look, Mr. Arturo, I'd like to share these beers with you, and these soft drinks are for the kids, since I know they don't drink, and I'd like to speak with your daughter, Johannes, just for a minute."

The old man let me unload all of that, but when I finished, he wouldn't let me in. He stood in front of the door like Barcelona's goalie and forcefully shook his head no. "This is a Christian family and we don't accept this kind of invitation." He said it just like that, strike me dead if I'm lying. That old coot was the biggest weirdo I've ever seen. Behind him was his wife, Carmen, who was almost as pretty as her daughter, but with a batty face that would give anyone the creeps. *Where did he get her from?* I thought. *A cave?* Anyway, I couldn't see Johannes until the next day, at the door to our school.

She was studying art at the city's art academy, the Benny Moré School, where she was the only black girl studying art; enough of her oil-colored kind were in music and dance, enough to make waves. I would go over there on my bicycle and they would look at me. *That's Gringo*, they'd think, *what a good-looking guy*, and they would come over to ask me, "Is that bicycle Italian? How many gears does it have?" I had a bunch of young black girls pining for me, and a few white ones, but to that Johannes, I didn't exist. *What a proud black girl*, I would think, *who does she think she is?* But the way she walked killed me, her agile gait that looked like she was dancing.

"You're losing it," Pork Chop told me. "That black girl is sharp, she won't suck off a black guy. Can't you see that she thinks she's better than anyone?"

"*Pinga*, don't be filthy, Piggy."

"The thing is, I need cash." He had already spent the ten thousand pesos I gave him after knocking off the *guajiro*. "We need to kill another one of these little cows . . . I have customers asking me, 'Come on, Salvador, if you get more veal like that, the really tender kind, the tourists were happy, we'll pay you double, but it has to be now that we're in peak season.' They're all coming after me, and I have to tell them to wait."

"You can tell that neither you nor they had to cut the guy up and make him into steaks. It's better to go to the countryside and kill a real cow."

"That's a lot of work . . . You have to walk a ton, and you can always get caught by a peasant. Besides, you have to carry off the meat in bags, which is really risky, and if they get you, they'll treat you just as if you offed some guy."

"Lower your voice, fucking Piggy. Or do you want everyone to hear you? If I get caught because of you, you'll be the one who ends up as tenderloin."

"No one's hearing a damned thing, everyone is here for the whores."

We were at el Ruso's bar, and one of his prettiest whores was dancing and showing off her tits. Pork Chop took a long drink, then gave me a piece of advice:

"If you want to conquer that Johannes, then you have to be more like her father . . . Become a Christian and that black girl is yours."

GUTS

I just didn't have a head for reading, it was hard as hell for me. I sat behind Cricket in class and I just wanted to fuck around; I couldn't stay still, I started to bob my knees up and down quickly until Magali, who sat at the same table I did, would say, "Guts, please sit still."

23

"If you show me your panties," I'd say, and she would lift the edge of her skirt, and I'd lower my head so I could take in her skinny legs, until the teacher stopped the lecture and said, "Whoever is not interested in what I'm saying can leave."

I would go out to the hallway and smoke a cigarette while I waited for snack time, then I would go home. I had threatened that teacher, whose last name was Suárez; once, I kept watch as he entered the teachers' bathroom and I pulled a knife on him because he'd been on my back, he'd gotten it into his gourd that I should repeat the eighth grade, he told everyone what was going to be on the tests except for me, he was really tough on me and had already failed me on the midterms. That day I pulled a knife on him, it was a madhouse, he started to shout and went running straight for the principal's office; I flew out of there to my house, the police came to get me, they put me in their patrol car, took me to the precinct, and there were the school principal and the teacher. They accused me of selling pornographic cards and of masturbating.

"Yohandris Carlos Fernández Ramírez is going straight to a juvenile detention center, where the real savages are, that's the place for him," said Pancho, the policeman, and signed a little piece of paper.

But the following day, my father called my uncle who sits on the Central Committee, and they sent me back to school. They even apologized, all the teacher could do was stand in front of the chalkboard and say I was the best thing since sliced bread; but I didn't have a head for reading, or for numbers. Cricket did. *That idiot knows so much*, I would think, and sometimes I felt like punching him. It sucks when you realize that a space cadet like that knows more than you.

"It's because he pays attention, Guts," said Nacho Fat-Lips, who had failed sixth grade for the second time.

"He doesn't pay shit. The point is that he has an engine in his head, and when it's running, he knows everything. All my head is good for is knocking people with it."

Despite his smarts, Cricket was pretty absentminded. Sometimes, he would just stand there, staring at the sun, oblivious to the world, he would even start drooling, and as tall and skinny as he was, he looked like something evil, like a wingless black heron wanting to fly. "Cricket," I would say, because he scared me when he got like that, and then he would start to sing, and that was the worst. "This one's nuts."

MARIBEL

There's very little to say about the mother. Since she almost never left the house, for the fifteen years she lived there, it would be a stretch if I said I talked to her a handful of times; she was, however, someone who shared, she didn't keep anything to herself. You just had to ask her for something for her to give it over, although later she would saddle you with one of those little sayings, Christian ones. I was really fucking sick of her Christianity.

GRINGO

I got tired of going everywhere on a bike, even though it was a good brand and everything, you had to pedal like hell, so I told Pork Chop, "My man, get things ready, 'cause early tomorrow, I'm going hunting. I don't want to see you drunk or poorly dressed; when I get to your house with the two-legged ox, everything has to be okay, is that clear?"

"Clear as water."

"Killing a guy is no easy thing, I'm doing this because we're in the *fuácata*, broke as hell, but if there were another way to make a living, really, I wouldn't do this."

"Me neither, chief," Pork Chop said. "I'd like to be good, not be messed up in anything, but what can you do, the money's gone."

"You said it."

That morning, I got dressed in the best I had, I waited until La Mimbre opened, and I stood really close to the door; every time I saw a well-dressed, big-time *guajiro*, I would whisper to him real low, "Wanna buy a motorbike?"

MARIANO MESA GUILLOT, *former principal of Rafael Espinosa High School*

The smart one was the younger one, Samuel Prince. His brother was only able to retain things, he had a fairly good memory, he was like a filter. But he was just an average student. Prince was brilliant. I taught both of them, and they had very different personalities. Cricket, or, rather, David King, just wanted to fit in, to get along with his classmates and be accepted; he participated in class and was pretty good at sports despite seeming uncoordinated because his limbs were so long. Samuel Prince, on the contrary, was proud, calculating. He never raised his hand, but when you addressed him, *Let's see, Samuel, tell us . . .* , he responded exhaustively. In physical education, he wasn't one of the worst, either, he could hold his own, especially in track and field, in endurance tests, no one could beat him. But when the trainers wanted to recruit him for the sports-focused high school, he said no. Anyway, I was the principal of that school for thirty straight years, and the best and the worst of everything passed through there, but what those Stuart boys did doesn't make any sense to me, it's like a sign of modern times, of what's to come, if I may. I can't connect those two young boys I met, whose heads I sometimes patted with my hand, with *that*; well, it takes my breath away, honestly.

Every person who is born into the world has the right to education and in return has the duty to contribute to the education of others, Martí said, and I tried to educate those young men, to give them a sense of what morals and ethics are, but I failed, because they were rotten. To the core, they were rotten; something was hiding behind that Christianity their parents paraded about—something.

MARIBEL

So Gringo is in a maximum-security prison in Texas, waiting to be wiped out? Now he can spend twenty years on death row because those *yanquis*, before they give someone the chair, they need to think about it a hundred times over, it's like they feel sorry for him. But Gringo was evil, evil, he was like a real Cro-Magnon. Do you know what it is to feed human flesh to half of Punta Gorda? I think of it and it turns my stomach, but at least he was considerate enough not to sell it here in the neighborhood; in that respect, he did exercise some control, because, you know, I said to him, "Hey, Gringo, old friend, come on, sell me a little piece and I'll pay you at the end of the month, I don't have anything to sink my teeth into, my molars are going to atrophy if I keep eating soy beef."

"Maribel, that meat's not good for you, you'll be allergic," he said to me the first time, and I kept pushing.

"Come on, old friend, get me a piece."

"Will you suck me off?"

"Sure."

But later he said it was a joke, so . . .

Gringo had a lot to do with what happened with the Stuarts. Since he was interested in Johannes, he became Christian. I saw him show up one day, dressed in clothes like I'd never seen him in before, a gray pair of dress pants and an ivory-colored woven shirt, waiting for the Stuarts to open the door so he could go to temple with them.

GRINGO

The old dumbass let me in; one afternoon, I went to the wood-shop where he worked, waited for him to come out, and went up to him.

"Mr. Stuart, I had a vision. I saw Jesus Christ come down a ladder surrounded by angels and say to me, 'Ricardo Mora Gutiérrez, be a good man, the day is near.'"

I had just bumped off my second two-legged ox and my pockets were stuffed with cash, so when the old man, after talking my ear off for two hours, told me that, regrettably, the Holy Sacrament of the Resurrected Christ had no temple in Cienfuegos, and that the contributions were few, I stuck my hand in my pocket, took out two twenty-dollar bills, and gave them to him right then and there.

"Thank you, may God bless you. Come by tonight, if you can, we're congregating at María Elizabet's house."

"I'll be there," I said to him.

It's not easy to take a guy out, and that second one wasn't as compliant as the first. He wasn't interested in motorcycles; he was a *guajiro* from Placetas, out in Villa Clara Province, who was looking for a plasma TV. When I told him about my cousin, the sailor who'd just returned from Panama, who had a sixty-four-inch Sony with a clock, USB port, built-in DVD, satellite system, and extended-range remote, he shook his head from side to side and said we should bring it to his friend's house, where he was staying.

"You've got to be crazy. Do you know how heavy a TV that size is, or are you playing dumb? Are you in or what?"

"Don't try that one on me, *mulato*; you were selling a motorcycle and now you also have a TV that's a dream. What are you playing at?"

"Everything and nothing, I have connections. I can even sell you a house on the Prado, an apartment in Pueblo Griffo, or an Alaskan husky, if you want. Do you want to see some dykes getting it on? Do you?"

"How much would that run me?"

"They're two girls from Havana who just got here. They're on the lam; they don't have a dime and are practically giving themselves away. For thirty dollars, you can see them get it on and fuck them both later."

"Damn, for that price, I can fuck seven times in my home-town, that's expensive."

"You don't know what you're talking about. This is first-class tail, one of them was Tosco's girlfriend. I bet you don't know who Tosco is."

"Of course I know. The musician."

"Bingo, but you're not man enough; go back to Placetas and keep fucking pigs."

"No need to get rude."

"Go to hell," I said to him, and turned my back, and then it was the guy coming after me.

"Don't get like that, *mulato*, let's go see the TV, and on the way I'll take a look at those chicks. They're not black, are they? Because, well, no offense, but I don't touch black girls."

"No way, they're both white; the only *mulata* is the other one."

"The other one?"

"Yeah, the one who was a model in Varadero, a *mulata* with green eyes and hair all the way down her back. But that one isn't into dykes."

"How much does that go for?"

"More or less the same."

"A black girl costs more than two white girls? No offense."

"That's the rate, what do you want me to do?"

"Talk to them, all my money is going to the TV."

"I don't know, you know how girls are. If I say something to them, they might think I want to pull a fast one, and then they blow me off and that's not good for me."

"Talk to them."

"Okay, but I'm not promising anything. Let's go," I said.

And he followed me like a lamb to Pork Chop's house. What he had in his pockets didn't even amount to a thousand dollars, of which I gave two hundred to Pork Chop, and we got another four thousand Cuban pesos for the meat because the guy was kind of skinny, although luckily he was tall and had good legs. When I pulled the Makarov on him, I couldn't keep him from screaming, but he let himself get tied up without a fuss and said to me, "I knew this was a con, that's what I get for doing business with you blacks, but I swear that I am going to look for you to the ends of the earth, and you're going to have to give me my money back."

"Who are you going to look for, kid?" I didn't say anything else because such naïveté filled me with pity.

I put a rag in his mouth, then sliced his throat. Pork Chop closed his eyes to keep from seeing the blood run out, so I said to him, as a joke, "If they ask you about the screams, tell them you were fucking."

"No one will hear anything," Pork Chop said. "Besides, it was a man's scream."

"Homos don't fuck?"

"Knock it off, Gringo."

I had to sell the bicycle to get the full amount, but the next morning I was at La Mimbre, trying out one of those motor scooters they make in Villa Clara. *It's funny*, I thought, *whatever I take from Villa Clara, I pay right back into its economy.*

ROGELIO ROCA CUEVA, *architect*

She didn't like Gringo, she was a real classy black girl, and although Gringo was a good-looking *mulato*, well-dressed, who'd swapped his bicycle for one of those motor scooters that hardly go but look really good—despite that she found

31

him ridiculous, she would look at him stone-faced and respond in monosyllables when he talked to her. I went to the Stuarts' house a lot back then, since Arturo had been named treasurer of the Holy Sacrament congregation and I was gathering funds to build the temple. After they got the permits from the mayor's office and the Department of Housing, they talked to me about designing the building, and they were punctilious, especially Stuart, who would show up to see me every once in a while at the provincial design office where I worked. Sometimes, he brought one of his children with him, usually the younger one, Prince, who back then was an easygoing kid; I think Gringo was the one who ruined him.

GRINGO

I never spoke to him about hunting down two-legged game or about con jobs, it's not like I was crazy; I only told him that he had to change, that he couldn't keep blindly believing that idiot father of his, that there was more to life than Christianity and Friday-afternoon fish dinners. I told him that because he was a brilliant kid, you could tell, despite his girliness, and because I knew what he had done to Barbarito, Lupe's kid, who was really just a useless shit. But, you know, he wasn't bad to begin with; I told him because I looked at him and thought, *This little black kid could end up being president if he sets his mind to it.*

GUTS

I wasn't born bad, what happened was that I didn't have a head for reading and I'd had several run-ins with the police, and when Pérez Roque and Carlos Lage came in, my uncle got left out of the Central Committee, so when I went to Ariza prison to see Nacho Fat-Lips, who had ended up there for taking a digital camera from an American lady, I told him, "Listen, Nacho, buddy, save a cot for me."

"I'll see what can be done, brother," he said. "Man, it's terrifying here. There are all these good-looking *bugarrones*, and I've got no reputation to protect me; I've got to keep one eye open when I sleep so no one gives it to me up the ass."

"Shit, man."

When I got to the neighborhood, I went to see Gringo. He was trying to pass as a Christian, but he didn't fool me. I waited until he arrived on that bank-manager motor scooter of his, and I went up to him.

"Listen, Gringuito, you were pals with my deceased brother, so I'm going to ask you a favor."

"Blessings. How much do you need?"

"Listen, Gringo, man, respect, but drop all that and talk to me straight, you don't need to put on that act with me."

"Okay then, talk to me."

"Gringo, *asere*, I'm this close to going to the hole, and I need some guidance. What can I do so I get respect and no one tries to fuck me up the ass?"

"Easy, you gotta kill someone. And not just anyone: someone who's been inside, and not just any ex-con, an old kingpin, a well-respected guy, that's the only way to go into Ariza with a reputation already."

"Damn, Gringo, you're a genius, thanks."

That's how I started to get screwed up. I told myself, *Guts, you're going to miss the girls and afternoon soccer games, but everyone has to follow his fate, just like Achilles in* The Iliad—*the only book worth reading, truth be told.*

ROGELIO

Around that time, a pastor from Oklahoma arrived. He was a tall black man, gray haired and round bellied; he went to the Stuarts' house and had a meeting with Basulto, the Holy Sacrament pastor in Cienfuegos, with Arturo and with me. I showed him the plans, he nodded and made just a few suggestions; what we couldn't agree on was the height of the roof, which he thought should be higher. Our people are charismatic, he said, then we all went to María Elizabet's, which, since she had been a piano teacher, had a big, tiled yard and a ton of plastic chairs; besides, the brothers in Christ brought whatever chairs were still needed, and at nine at night, when the whole congregation was gathered, the guy from Oklahoma addressed us in pretty clear Spanish. He said it was the first time he'd come to Cienfuegos, but he knew Arturo Stuart from the three times he had been in Camagüey, and we should be happy that a gentleman of such virtue was among us, not to ignore, of course, other sober gentlemen like Ángel Basulto, who, despite his youth, fulfilled to perfection his work as pastor . . . We should also be thankful for the fine ladies who, led by Carmen Stuart, helped the men carry out good works and the construction of the temple.

"While I'm on the subject, your brothers over at the Holy Sacrament church in Oklahoma hereby donate this modest amount," the American concluded, and he deposited in Basulto's hands a round lump that the latter immediately passed on to Arturo Stuart, who was the treasurer.

"Ten thousand dollars is but a small sum to demonstrate our love for you," the American said, and from the nearly one thousand mouths of those gathered at María Elizabet's house came a categorical sigh of admiration.

GRINGO

I was there when that old black goat donated the ten thousand dollars, I saw how Arturo Stuart opened the envelope and showed us one hundred hundred-dollar bills. My mouth watered, but I stood up and applauded with the rest of them. Then everyone just had to testify; that is, to reveal Christ's life-changing power, and the greatest testimony there, of course, was mine.

"Here we have Ricardo Mora Gutiérrez, also known as Gringo, a young man who was following the wicked path of sorcery, who abused alcohol, drugs, was violent, and who was involved in illegal activity, and now thanks to the power of the Word, he ceased to be Gringo in order to be only Ricardo, our brother in God." All of that was said in one breath by that Basulto, the pastor, a useless shit who wasn't worth even half my fist; and then he said, "But let's allow him to be the one who speaks to us of his experience."

So I had to stand up and walk to the center and tell, for the thousandth time, how I had dreamed of baby Jesus and angels coming down a staircase made all of marble and then, blah-blah-blah, thanks to Brother Arturo Stuart, who guided me, blah-blah-blah, in the bosom of the Lord, blah-blah-blah, I found peace. I even got to feeling happy after letting out that gibberish, since I felt like I was practically Stuart's son-in-law, and I looked at Johannes and it seemed to me that something beautiful was in her eyes as she looked at me. Later, I told Pork Chop about it.

"Piggy, *asere*, that chick is starting to love me."

"That's great. Pretty soon, you'll have her. But can I ask you a favor without you getting mad, eh, my friend?"

"Go ahead."

"*Asere*, don't call me Piggy anymore. My name is Salvador Betancourt, and if that seems too long to you, call me Pork Chop, *vaya*."

We were at el Ruso's bar with a Bucanero beer in front of each of us, Piggy dressed almost as nicely as I was, in brand-name jeans, a brand-name shirt, and a pair of Adidas on his hooves.

"Piggy you are and Piggy you'll be," I enunciated. "And if you don't like it, deal with it."

"You're fucking impossible, *asere*."

"Don't you know it."

"We've got to take out another one."

"Oh, really, so who's going to do it? You?"

"Brother, you know I'm not smooth enough for that, my thing is going to Punta Gorda for you and handing out steaks."

"So you're going to waste him."

"I can't, man, really, why should I lie to you? I don't see myself sticking a knife in anyone; I'm too slow for that."

"So you can't take a guy out, but you spend money like it's water. Don't tell me you're broke?"

"I have a lot of expenses."

"Yeah, screwing around with whores and getting drunk. Save something for a rainy day, this can't go on forever."

"If you say so, Gringo."

"Well, what do you think? That I'm going to spend my days sending Christians to meet their maker? If I do it again, it'll be 'cause this little motor scooter is rubbing my ass raw, I want a real motorcycle . . . But we'll discuss that later, 'cause today, I'm happy. You know, Piggy, that chick is starting to notice me."

"You think, Gringo?"

A few days ago, that fat minister from Oklahoma came to see me here, on death row. He brought me a Bible with a black cover that I placed with the others, cigarettes, and one of those lemon bars that are an American specialty. I would have preferred he bring me a novel, even if it was in English, but that's not how these guys from the Holy Sacrament are. At least he entertained me for a while and brought back memories of my time in Cuba. He ended up asking me if I regretted anything. Everything, of course, I said to him, and he smiled in great satisfaction, I was telling him what he wanted to hear, that's how they are. But when he was leaving, I said to him, "I'm still devoted to Palo." Of course, he didn't really understand, but he could tell it was nothing good.

The Devil looks after his own, and in the end, something will happen, and they won't end up giving it to me, the lethal injection they put in your veins will spoil, and instead they'll pump me full of heroin—I don't know, but something will come up. If Pork Chop were here, I would tell him, *Piggy, I got screwed over because of love, because of love I started snuffing out* guajiros *and then I developed a taste for it.*

Pork Chop would say, *Nah, you're here because you were born bad, see how in the land of gringos they don't call you Gringo anymore, now they say you're Satan. You could have been the wise-guy who went furthest in the neighborhood if not for the Stuart brothers; although you were the one who taught Jelly, and he was the worse of the two.*

That's what fucking Piggy would say, and it's a lie, I wasn't anybody's teacher, I only wanted to help him earn respect be-cause I saw potential in him, he was the one who asked me one day, "What about those cuts on your arm, what are they, Ricardo? Can you explain them to me?"

We were sitting in the living room at his house, his mother was puttering about the kitchen. Neither his father nor Jo-hannes nor Cricket were at home, but I delayed a second any-way before I answered, "The thing is, I've been initiated into Palo, Prince, into Palo."

"What's that, Ricardo? Explain it, please."

"I'll tell you, Prince, if you promise not to tell anyone, es-pecially not your parents, or Johannes."

"Not even Johannes?"

"Not even her. Your sister kind of looks down on me, and, my man, it weighs on me."

"She's like that, don't mind her. Come on, tell me, I prom-ise not to say anything."

"Okay. Look, Palo is the natural religion for us black folks because, Prince, listen, there's a spirit in everything."

"Do you think so? My father says there's just one God, and that not even a hair on my head moves without His authority."

"And you believe him? Your father isn't the sharpest tool

38

in the shed, he spends all day covered in grease and sawdust. Look at me: young, everyone calls me *sir*, I've got a motor scooter and a pile of cash and tons of chicks chasing after me . . . Speaking of chicks, I don't want you to get mad, young Prince, but are you a queer or not? Tell me, and believe me, if you say yes, I'm not going to care, everyone moves to his own beat."

"No, I'm not a queer, at least, I don't think so."

"So then, you should know that to get girls, you have to let go of all that nonsense."

"I know, that's why I want to keep studying, so I can get away from all this shit."

JUAN PABLO SOSA ROMERO, *painter and engraver from Cienfuegos*

Around then, I started dating Johannes. Ever since she started at the school, I'd noticed her, I liked how her hand moved quickly over the paper as she outlined a drawing, I liked the way she talked, and that in addition to being pretty and talented, she wasn't full of herself, rather, she was simple, sometimes too simple. What I didn't like was her weird family, her father and mother with God always on the tips of their tongues, and those brothers . . . From the beginning, they seemed certifiable. I was really leaning toward sculpture, but to be closer to her, I started spending more time on oil painting. We had a teacher, Juan Francisco, who was very sociable, and sometimes when almost everyone else had gone, we would be left alone with him, each of us at our respective easels, and although we barely spoke, I felt at peace.

ROGELIO

She took to hanging out with a white guy who had long hair, jeans that were ripped at the knee, and tattoos on both arms. Ever since the father saw him, he said the kid was satanic, and that if she kept hanging out with that little *roquero*, he would take her out of art school, he'd never agreed with her being there anyway, what a young woman should study is something practical, economics or to be a secretary, artists starve to death. Arturo Stuart himself told me all this the afternoon we were laying down the concrete for the new church.

GRINGO

He asked me, "Why do they call you Gringo?"

"Because I wear threads that only Americans wear, brand-name clothes, so people respect me, and when they see me, they say, 'There goes a classy black man,' instead of 'There goes a black man with no class,' you get it? If it weren't so damned hot here, I would walk around in a suit with a silk tie, like Denzel Washington, because I'm not some lowlife, Prince, not some lowlife, I've got a name."

"What's that mean?"

"I get respect."

"Ah."

"Do you want to get respect?"

"Sure."

"Not sure. Yes or no?"

"Yes."

"You have to start now when you're still just a boy, because to be respected, you have to learn a lot. Go where men are, not those church mice, and stop being such a sissy."

"Okay, take me."

"First you have to promise you won't tell anyone."

"Promise."

"And what did your sister say?"

"Nothing. That she likes you, but she doesn't want a boy-friend now."

"What would she like as a gift for Valentine's Day?"

"I don't know . . . a visual-arts book, by Leonardo da Vinci, maybe . . . ?"

JUAN PABLO

One day she said to me, "This is over," and that was it. That's why I say she was like her father, decisive. I didn't understand, she could've explained to me, she could've told me that neither of us was getting much out of it. My family had come to accept her, they didn't care that her skin was so dark. My ma was already dreaming of having a pair of beautiful biracial grand-children, tall ones, because Johannes and I are tall and slim. I think her father pressured her, and that crazy guy, Gringo, who gave me dirty looks, even though I told him I was only going to Johannes's house to study. Now I understand that I was lucky as all hell because that animal would've killed me just like he killed those people. In sum, I think that what most influenced the end of my relationship with Johannes were two other things: first, that we didn't jive sexually, the four or five times we slept with each other, she didn't orgasm. I wasn't man enough for her, I realize, and Johannes is the kind of woman who, you might not think it, needs to be fulfilled in bed; that's why, when they told me that she married her first Italian for ulterior motives, I didn't say a word; at the end of the day, I'm a discreet man, but I thought they were mistaken, very mistaken. Back when we were dating, I was already living in this big house, in the middle of the Prado in Cienfuegos, with just my parents, and she could have perfectly well come to live with us, my mother would have welcomed her perfectly. But no, she preferred to keep living on that alleyway in Punta Gotica with her two brothers in addition to their parents, a place where she practically had to use the roof in order to paint because there was so little space, all because she didn't love me enough, at least not as a boyfriend, since we remained friends until she left . . . and that last reason is the second and, to me, most important cause for our relationship's failure, the fact that she always knew she was going to leave all this shit behind and she didn't want any sad memories.

"To Havana?" I asked the first time she said that to me.

"No, away from *here*. I'm going to really leave."

"Let's leave together, I have an aunt in the U.S., I'll talk to her and she'll claim me."

"No," she said. "I'm not going to lift boxes for some shop or take care of old folks or work as a waitress, I'm not cut out for any of that. I'm going as a painter, I'm going to make it as an artist, and for that, I need to be alone, I don't want anyone distracting me."

She laid this on me three days before definitively breaking up with me, and I thought she was dreaming, because few artists in the world manage to make a living from their creations, but later it turns out that I was the one who was mistaken, now she's famous. Yesterday, while looking at used books, I saw a magazine from last year where they talked about the future marriage of the well-known Italian artist of Cuban origins, Judith Alonso, to a soccer player from Naples, a Vicente or Vicenzo. In the article, it specified that this guy had just signed a contract with Real Madrid, and the *tifosi*, who were not happy at all, vowed to go to Monte Carlo, where the nuptials would take place, to make trouble; regarding the visual artist, they didn't say much more, but, paying attention to the photo, I again saw Johannes, she was still very much like she was here in Cienfuegos, just lighter, discolored, she could almost pass for olive skinned. "You can tell she doesn't get any sun," my mother said to me, since I bought the magazine and took it to her so she could see where the girl who could have been her daughter-in-law ended up. "But she's thinner," my mother kept saying, and that her dress didn't suit someone her age, she wasn't a princess or anything of the sort. I know my mother said this last thing to console me since Johannes looked beautiful, and although I didn't love her anymore and don't even know if I ever did love her, or if all there was between us was puppy love, she had achieved her dream and I was still stuck here, making sculptures of ballplayers and old musicians, works of drab realism that brought in money for me but didn't take me anywhere, participating in second-rate contests and aspiring to be remembered one day and to receive the Machete of the Southern Mambí or la Roseta, symbols of the city of Cienfuegos.

"Have you spied on your sister, Cricket?"

"That's a sin."

"Says who? Your dad? That geezer's a fairy and your brother is also a fairy and you're also kind of a fairy."

"Don't fuck around or I'll cut your dick off."

"It's a joke, Cricket, but you really haven't spied on Johannes?"

"Of course not, she's my sister."

"If she wasn't your sister, would you spy on her?"

"I don't know, maybe . . . Do you spy on your sister, Guts?"

"Yeah, of course, and I jerk off; after all, she has no idea."

"You're a sicko and a sinner."

"Yeah, but I enjoy it . . . Let's go spy on her, come on, come with me."

"I said no, it's a sin."

"Not your sister, or mine. Berta, who's coming home from school now and bathes nude in the corridor behind her house, you'll see what kind of snatch she has."

"But what if we get caught?"

"We're not going to get caught."

"How do you know?"

"I know. Let's go up to the roof of your house and you'll see that we won't get caught."

"But what if we get caught? If my mom tells *el puro*, the old man will kill me . . . Look what he did to me."

"Damn, your old man is crazy as hell, and that's with him being a Christian."

"You don't know the half of it."

"What'd he do that to you with?"

"With his belt. Can't you see the shape of his belt buckle?"

"Fuck, if that were me, I'd kill him."

"He's my father."

"Well, that's on you. Do we go spying or not?"

"Let's go."

MARIBEL

I would hear her shout, *Arturo, let him go. Arturo, please, that's enough!* That was only sometimes, since usually all I could hear was a muffled sound like someone shaking out a rug, that and the kid whimpering. He never hit the other one, Jelly; it was the strangest thing in the world. Once I dared ask Carmen if the three of them had the same father.

"Of course," she said, "whose would they be?"

"So why does one of them get so many beatings while the other doesn't see as much as a rose petal lifted against him? Even the girl gets smacked every once in a while, but Prince . . . it's not like he's a saint."

"You just happen to know what goes on at my house?"

"No, Carmen, I'm sorry."

She gave me that dead little mosquito face that didn't affect me at all.

This one has her wits about her, I thought. *What could they have done in Camagüey? Because it had to have been something major for them to run away from that city and end up burying themselves here in* la cuartería, *these squalid rooming houses, something major.*

45

He looked like a stick, I mean his body, all fiber and bones; his face also looked like a stick, with that grimace of disgust that seldom changed, like you owed him something. *Blessings*, he would say as his only greeting, and it seemed as if the one doing the blessing was him, not God. He gave off a sense of violence, although at first glance, he seemed like a gentle guy, very gentle. He almost always had his Bible in his hands, as if the Gospels were his shield. He was the one who decided on the location of the church, over my criteria as an architect. He drew Basulto in and filled his head with smoke. I told him:

"Basulto, this is the Church of the Holy Sacrament for all of Cienfuegos, not just the neighborhood of Punta Gotica; I've been an architect for twenty years, and if you're not going to listen to me, find someone else."

I left the architectural plans on the dining room table, grabbed my bicycle, and went home. There was a knock at my door an hour later. *Blessings*, a voice said dryly.

"Blessings," my wife said. "Come in, Arturo. Would you like some water?"

"Yes, please, it's so hot."

My wife went to get the water, and I came out of my room and shook Stuart's hand. Then we sat down in the rocking chairs, and when he'd drunk the water, he started to tell us how important it was for a neighborhood like Punta Gotica, a neighborhood of forgotten black people and desperate white people, to have that church right in the center, where everyone could see it; then he got straight to the point:

"Two hundred pesos per day," he said, looking around at my large but run-down house.

"What do you mean?"

"You heard me."

That's how he was, always with God on the tip of his tongue, but convinced that everything could be resolved through money and demagoguery. He was pretty talkative. Almost everyone who worked on that temple did so for free, as volunteers.

GRINGO

"Listen," Piggy said to me when I'd just gotten to el Ruso's bar. "They're asking around about a certain Aramís Ramírez."

"What's that to me?"

"He's from Cabaiguán."

"Who's asking?"

"A *mulato* in a checked shirt who looks like a cop."

"Let him ask. Give him some space to ask about whatever he wants, he's not gonna know which end is up, no one here knows a thing."

"No, not here, but lots of people in San Lázaro must have seen that big *guajiro* when you took him to my house."

"Nobody remembers that, Piggy, don't be a drag."

"The thing is, while you're out there on your motor scooter doing favors for the church, I'm the one who has to face the issues."

"Are you high or what the fuck is wrong with you? Watch how you talk to me."

"The thing is, the money ran out, Gringo, and I'm in the *fuácata*. Throw me a bone, come on."

"I'm starting to think you eat cash for dinner. Start saving, *asere*, start saving."

ROGELIO

The unfinished temple of the Holy Sacrament is the only remnant of Arturo Stuart's time in Cienfuegos, and it's enough. I'm proud of that temple; sometimes when I'm in the mood, I get on my bicycle and go see it. It's in ruins, but continues to be a beautiful building. The only fruit of my twenty years of labor as an architect. There isn't a single piece of marble or bronze stating the name of the architect who designed it; in another twenty years no one will remember me, and it will be as if the temple erected itself; perhaps that's fair, because that cathedral is cursed.

I don't walk with God anymore, now I go it alone, I no longer tell anyone that an angel without wings suggested the shape of the temple to me. He said, *My church will be like this*, and he lifted me on his back and I saw the Cienfuegos of the future, a beautiful city, full of elegant buildings, and cleaner than ever, and in Punta Gotica, I saw a futuristic building, with many stained-glass rose windows, and that was the temple. *Cienfuegos is the celestial Jerusalem*, I thought, awoke, and my wife had to wash the sheets; I had wet the bed like when I was a child.

The next day, I arrived with my architectural plans at Stuart's house. Basulto was there, along with many members of the congregation and, of course, the owner of the house.

Every neighborhood where poor people live looks the same; in fact, they are the same: sewers that overflow when it rains, streets full of potholes, and walls papered over with advertising. The six months I spent in downtown Miami felt as if I'd never been able to leave Punta Gotica, so one day I said to myself, "I didn't get myself out of Cienfuegos to keep being a second-class citizen."

I spoke basic enough English, but had too strong an accent, so I spent some of the dollars I had left on perfecting my language. That was during my first days in America, as the *yumas* call that fucking country.

Yesterday afternoon, a journalist, a Pulitzer Prize winner, came for me to tell him my life story; he was going to pay me ten thousand dollars up front, and if the book sold well, we'd both end up millionaires because these are the kinds of stories that Americans like. "Start from the beginning," he told me.

I had to laugh. "What do I need money for when I'm already on death row?"

He asked me whether I didn't have a relative in Cuba, or in the U.S., to whom I could leave the money.

"No. I don't have anyone, just Lucy, my ex-wife, and that damn bitch hasn't come to see me a single time."

"Well, then . . . ," the journalist pressed on. He was a short, kind of fat guy, of Salvadoran origins, according to what he'd told me before. "The book could be in your best interest. You know how the Americans are, maybe they'll sympathize with a childhood like yours, plagued by hardship, and pressure the state's governor, I don't know . . ."

"How do you know my childhood was plagued by hardship? Are you psychic?"

"It's always like that. Childhood makes us what we are."

"No: I was screwed over by love. I was a good-looking *mulato* selling sunglasses and brand-name clothing at the door of Cienfuegos's best store, La Casa Mimbre. I made easy money and sometimes lent it out at high interest, making some extra cash. I was great until a family of dark-skinned blacks moved in and I met the most beautiful woman in the world; I was screwed over because of her, it's because of her that I started doing what I did."

"What is it that you did?"

"What am I going to tell you for? Knowing what I did in the U.S. is already more than enough for you. Just know that man is like the wolf, when his thirst for killing is unleashed, there's nothing more to be done, there's no going back."

"You're still a good-looking man," the guy threw at me in English, all of a sudden, and I had to tell him in the same language that I'm no fudge packer, something that made my favorite guard, Billy Holden—a black guy who is six foot two and two hundred pounds—start laughing.

"I'm telling you because our magazine is willing to pay you to pose in the nude; you don't know how many female admirers you have here in Texas," the guy clarified, looking at me through the bulletproof glass, scratching his chin with the phone.

"Yes, I do know," I told him. "I get a lot of letters. They think I'm a sex symbol because I married all those hags and then snuffed them out."

GUTS

"Fuente Ovejuna, señor" is one of the few things I remember from my whole time in school; of course, I know how to read, write, count, and everything else, but really, I didn't have a brain for reading and that worries me. "Could I be slow?" I ask myself at times, and then I say, no, because I escaped like Jonah from the whale, I'm living an okay life here in Barcelona, and that's with all the bad things I did in my Cuban days. I remember that when I lived in Punta Gotica, all I wanted was a white girl. *Dear God*, I would pray, *let her run around on me as much as she wants, but give me a white girl, not a* mulata *or an Indian girl, or an olive-skinned girl, give me one of those white girls whose veins show through her skin; come on, God, and of course, let her be hot.* In Cuba, that kind of chick is in short supply. In my class, only one girl was like that, she lived on the Prado and had an Irish mother. Here, I'm surrounded by blondes and by legs, those Catalan women have some legs! In Cuba, to see hot white girls, you had to go spying on them in Punta Gorda. I would tell Cricket, *Get it together and let's go, we've got a show tomorrow*, and at the beginning, he would start with the buts: *But we're going to get caught. But, come on, I'm Christian. But . . .* Then he developed a liking for it and he was the one who invited me.

MARIBEL

Everyone knew Cricket was a Peeping Tom, but nobody cared. Almost all the young kids here spy on women, and you can let them or not, depending on whether you like the person looking. I let him sometimes because I knew how much he was working on building that crazy temple his father was making and I felt bad for him. *Go on, look and have yourself a good time*, I would think when I heard his soft steps on the roof, and if it was hot, I would grab my little bucket of water and go bathe in the corridor behind my home, then I would remove my clothing deliberately and start to pour the water over myself slowly to please him, I would take all the time in the world to soap up my tits, then my legs; of course, I wasn't the old crow I am now, I was a full-bodied *mulata*, I was forty years old, but you had to treat me with respect; later, I got diabetes and it's doing away with me, there's no slowing it down. They say that in the *Yuma* there are some little pills that cure you right away, but I don't have any family there, and Gringo's on death row, so if I ask him for those pills, he's probably going to tell me to go to hell.

GRINGO

The day before his birthday, I said to him, "What kind of present do you want?" He told me, "You don't have to give me anything, Ricardo, your friendship is enough." But I pressed him, "Come on, use that mouth of yours, ask me. An iPod? Don't be shy."

"Take me to see your *Padrino*."

"What?"

"You heard me."

"Okay, if you say so. Let me set up the meeting and I'll let you know."

GUTS

I saw him with Gringo everywhere. *Gringo's fucking him*, I thought at first, but no, because he looked even more macho than ever. *Gringo became Christian for real and they're going around with their Jesus Christ bullshit and all that*, I thought, but Gringo spent his nights at el Ruso's bar drinking whiskey and looking at tits. *Getting together that much with someone like Gringo, the worst kind of bad, that's not good for such a fresh-faced, delicate kid*, I thought. *He's just getting his ass ready, if not for Gringo, who never seemed like much of a* bugarrón, *then for someone else, maybe Salvador Piggy, that guy really doesn't care whether it's a woman, a dog, a transvestite, or a banana tree, he just wants to stick it in some hole.*

ROGELIO

"Ornament is crime," a great architect said, and that was my premise, I wanted the building to be perfect in its almost necessary simplicity, I wanted all of its complexity to come from the harmony and the quality of the materials used, I wanted to bring a piece of modernity to a sleepy Cuban town, I wanted that filthy neighborhood of Punta Gotica to have at least one thing to show the world, and I made an effort to achieve this.

"We had something else in mind, I don't know, something more traditional," Basulto said to me, and showed me a picture of the Church of the Holy Sacrament in Oklahoma, where the officiant was the Reverend James Harrison Fitzgerald, the corpulent black pastor who had done so much to collect the money we needed to build.

I hadn't slept all night and was somewhat irritable.

"If I have to redraft this, it's over, find another architect."

"It's not that we don't like it," Arturo Stuart said. "It's that it's so different, and it looks very expensive. Besides, where are you going to find the workers to do something like this? In Cuba, there aren't builders who do this kind of work anymore, the mosaics alone would be a headache."

"The materials and the workmen will appear."

"Yes, but at what cost?" Basulto said. "We only have twenty thousand dollars, and money doesn't grow on trees."

"Is this the entrance?" Stuart pointed at something on the architectural plan laid out on the table.

"You can access the temple's interior many ways. The concept is accessibility, permission, the temple is like an open hand everyone can hold . . . Perhaps you can see it better on the perspective drawing," I said, "but I didn't have time to finish it."

"So do it," Stuart said. "Do it and bring it over, and then we'll talk."

GRINGO

Knock, knock, they banged on the door, and I knew it was the police. I opened up and there they were: a fat *mulato* with a checked shirt and the sector chief.

"Blessings," I said to them, and smiled widely. "Come in and sit down."

They sat on the sofa and I took a seat facing them, in one of the armchairs.

"You're really thriving, Ricardo Mora Gutiérrez," the sector chief said. "This looks like a showroom, you're living better than Rockefeller. Don't tell me you started working, because all you're good for is construction and that doesn't pay much. What are you involved with, Ricardo Mora, huh?"

"Nothing. I converted, now I follow the path of the Lord."

"Really? How nice. How long ago did that conversion happen?"

"Nine months ago."

"Nine months? Sounds like a pregnancy," the sector chief said, and let out a tiny laugh like a sad hyena.

"In a way, it is, God is something that fills you."

"Gringo the Christian, well, well, this is something you wouldn't see anywhere else."

"Now you know. Would you like coffee?"

"Why not? Bring a cup for each of us, but don't you spit in it."

"I wouldn't dare." I went to brew the coffee.

When I returned, the sector chief asked me how much the living room set had cost me.

"I got it cheap, five hundred."

"That's a steal. Who makes it? So I can buy myself one, give me the telephone number or the address."

"That's in dollars."

"Well then, you should have started there. That's a lot of money. I've never seen that much all together and, you know, I work hard . . . Where'd you get it from, Gringuito? Don't tell me you won the lottery."

"My brother sent me the money."

"Damn, your brother's a really nice guy."

"Now you know."

"And here I was, thinking he left and never wrote to you again."

"He decided it's never too late to go to school. He got a degree as a nurse and works at one of the best hospitals in Miami, and he's decided to help me."

"What a brother, he's pure gold."

"We were always very close."

"You don't need to say so, you used to kill cows together."

"If you say so . . . Excuse me, the coffee's almost ready."

"How do you know?"

"I can smell it."

"With a nose like that, you should become a policeman, Gringuito . . . But go, I don't want your coffeemaker to blow up . . ."

"So delicious," the sector chief said later, when he sipped his coffee. "You must be asking yourself what we're doing here at your house. Right?"

"Of course."

"You can't think of anything?"

"I'm not psychic."

"Ah, you're not psychic . . . Well then, I'm going to help you. We're looking for an individual, from Santiespíritu, folks say they saw him with you."

"With me?"

BERTA

On February 27, 2007, the ghost started to torment me. The first time I saw him, seated at the entrance to *la cuartería*, he was looking ahead in concentration, as if he were waiting for

56

something. I knew he was dead because his eyes were rolled back and he was naked. It was nearly six in the evening, the time when kids are playing soccer and the street is full of adults coming back from work or going to their businesses. No one noticed. Only I saw him and his strong body; he had a scorpion tattooed on his right shoulder and a snake around his belly button, he was tall and would have been handsome without the open wound crossing his neck from one end to the other. He pointed at the wound with the index finger of his right hand and his eyes full of tears. I started to run.

I didn't eat that day.

"A naked dead man appeared to me," I told my mother.

"You and your jokes."

"I'm serious."

"So tell him to come cook for us, you don't know how to do anything and I'm pretty tired of the stink of grease."

Don't run, my name is Aramís and I'm from Cabaiguán, he said to me the second time I saw him, on a steamy Tuesday. I was at school and had asked the chemistry teacher for permission to go to the bathroom. I'd just sat down on the toilet when he appeared and said that. All I could do was look at him and say, *You don't exist*, then I closed my eyes, and when I opened them, he was no longer there. When I returned to the classroom, I was so pale, I looked like Michael Jackson.

"I was going to send someone for you," the teacher said. "I thought you'd gone down the toilet."

"I don't feel good. I saw a dead person."

"You can tell," he said with a smile, but then he let me leave.

I went home, made the most of my mom's not being there,

took two diazepam, swallowed them, sat on one of the rocking chairs in the living room, and rocked until the pills began to take effect; then, when I couldn't keep my eyes open, I went to lie down and in my bed was the dead man.

"My name is Aramís and I'm from Cabaiguán. I came to Cienfuegos looking for a motorcycle because I wanted to surprise Araceli, who wanted to see me on a motorcycle, but as you can see, they killed me and I can't figure out how to return to my town and tell them I'm dead; I went to the station but I can't get on a bus; when I try boarding, the bus turns to smoke and I find myself again in the house where they did this to me."

The dead man took his hand to his throat and then implored:

"Help me."

IBRAHIM

In spite of everything, those days were good; my wife would make my coffee; after drinking it, I would grab my bicycle and go to the temple. No matter how early it was, brother Arturo would already be there doing something: organizing the work tools or tidying up. We would pray together and await the arrival of our other brothers in Christ, the architect and the bricklayers, in order to have breakfast and begin the day's tasks. Ibrahim is a Syrian name, and everyone has always referred to me as the Arab, even though I don't have people in the Islamic lands: I was named Ibrahim after a telenovela that my mother saw years ago.

"Don't you sleep, maestro?" I once asked.

Stuart looked at me with those deep eyes of his that, in spite of everything, I dare to call those of a prophet, and said, "*Árabe*, when the church is done, I'll sleep so much that everyone in my house will think I've died."

To raise a temple up where there was nothing but weeds, to see it grow, take shape, go from being four stakes in the ground to a building whose walls rise each day . . .

At the beginning, they mocked us, and even though we had all the necessary permits possible, the police and inspectors came to harass us. When we were in full swing, they called the architect and told him we had to stop and look for all the receipts proving we'd acquired the cement through official means and not illegally. Then Rogelio had to bike to his house to look for the receipts and show them, otherwise we couldn't continue. Another day, they'd ask about bricks, the paint, about whatever they could, and there were many inspectors, so they took turns. One of the ones who fought with us most was a short little lady, chubby, who always wore a handkerchief on her head. She would arrive on a motor scooter like Gringo's, stand close to everything, open a black folder, pull out a planner, and start taking notes with her eyes fixed on us. She tried to make us nervous, but she couldn't anymore because the spirit of the Lord was with us. We sang hymns to Christ as we worked. Especially the one that says, "Christ has risen." Many of the neighbors accompanied us, and some of them worked with us, although we had to take many precautions because as soon as you let your guard down, they could take one of your work tools, a can of paint, half a bag of cement, whatever, all to resell it for moonshine.

"Yes, with you . . . I'm going to refresh your memory: he was alone, white, tall, strong, about twenty-five years old."

"Ah, that one . . . That guy left the country, a speedboat came to get him."

"How do you know?"

"He told me so. 'I'm leaving,' he said, 'and you won't see any trace of me again.'"

"Oh, yeah? So what did he go see you for?"

"He was looking for my brother's address, since they knew each other from when my *bróder* lived in Cabaiguán, and he wanted to meet up with him in Miami."

"So did you give it to him?"

"Of course I didn't, my brother has enough problems already without having to take care of some dumbass from Santiespíritu."

Both guys looked at me for a few seconds without saying anything, then the *mulato* said, "He's lying. Aramís would never leave the country, he was a hardworking, well-integrated young man, from a family with an impeccable record. I very much doubt that he would have known the brother from here. Besides, what person, living close to the northern coast, would think of coming down to Cienfuegos to leave Cuba?"

"I said the same thing to him. 'Brother,' I said, 'isn't it better for you to leave through Sagua la Grande, just a quick hop from Miami?' And he said that it was bad up there, the border guards were on high alert and the trip cost twice as much."

"He told his family he was going to Cienfuegos to buy a motorcycle."

"That was his story, but really, he was taking off."

"And he came and told you when you'd barely met?"

"Now you know."

"How strange," the *mulato* said.

"Not just strange, superstrange," said the other one. "There's something fishy here. So where were you and Aramís going when you were seen?"

"Over to see some chicks. He was a fan of the *mulatas*."

"Chicks? What chicks? Name and address."

"I would give it to you, but one of them is married."

"Well, well, out looking for chicks . . . Didn't you just tell me that you were Christian?"

"So Christians don't fuck?"

"Of course they do, Gringuito, of course they do . . . Okay, so you saw the chicks, and then?"

"He went on his way and I went mine."

"And which way did he go?"

"That, I can't tell you."

"Why not?"

"Because I don't know."

"You never know anything."

IBRAHIM

He was a good speaker, if you ask me, he was a better preacher than the pastor, and he had such a good memory that he could cite all the Scripture without making a mistake, and that was at just shy of fifteen years old. But something was off about him, something bad, he was proud, he thought he was predestined for something big, and that made him difficult to deal with, he

61

barely collaborated on building the temple. His brother, just a year older, did work like an ox even though his father was merciless with him, he treated him as if he hated him, as if the kid should pay daily for not being perfect. I didn't like that and one day I told him so. We were placing the fourth row of bricks. David King, who was working as an assistant of mine, dropped one of those bricks, which only broke in one corner, and his father became so furious that he practically went mad:

"Do you know how much those bricks cost?" he yelled.

"No, *papá*."

"So then be more careful."

"Yes, *papá*."

"It could happen to anyone," I said.

"When I want your opinion, I'll ask for it," old Stuart said to me, and got in my face, it was as if he were going to hit me there in front of everyone. He was like that, calm on the surface but with a barely contained rage ready to come out at any moment.

GRINGO

I wanted to bring her with me, even if I had to pay twice as much for the boat trip. *I'll get the money back*, I thought, and sometimes I think of how different my life would have been if Johannes had said to me, *I'm going with you*, when I proposed it to her, maybe I wouldn't be here waiting to meet my maker, maybe I would have blended in and become one of those guys who put little American flags on the hoods of their cars and grill on Sunday afternoons, and later there they are, all fat, beer in hand, arguing with the neighbors about the World Series.

If I had taken Johannes with me, everything would have been different, I'm sure, I wouldn't have gotten myself in a mess; maybe I would have done well, because to get ahead here, you don't have to bump anyone off, what you need here above anything else is someone to love you, and, ah, someone you can love, which is even harder. If that afternoon, when she was coming back from her school weighed down with poster board and paintbrushes, Johannes had played along when I said to her, "Let's go sit down in Martí Park, we have to talk," and then once we were there and I asked if she wanted a beer, since I had so much to tell her, if at that moment she had said, *Yes, bring me a beer*, and if she had smiled at me, my life would be different now, I'm sure of it, but that Johannes said no to the beer, and later, no matter how much I talked to her, she kept refusing:

"No, Ricardo, I'm not abandoning my future for you, or for anyone."

"What future do you have in this shitty country? Besides, I love you, do you know that? Because of you, I changed and now I'm someone else."

"I only like you as a friend, Ricardo, I've tried so many ways to make you understand. That's how things are and they can't be changed, I'm sorry."

That's how these bitches are, women, they're always sorry, they rip your heart out and then they're sorry, simple as that. I don't trust any of them anymore. I don't even trust my mother, that's the truth. The other day, a ghost appeared to me, it came from Cuba, to ask me why I had killed him when he was in the prime of his life.

"That's how it is, you go around doing as much damage

as you can until it's your turn for the coffin to drop, and you know, my time has come, I have just days left, so don't worry, soon you'll be happier; but when I'm dead, I don't ever want to see you; if I see you there on the other side, I'm going to give you the kind of beating that everyone but you will enjoy."

That's what I said to him, because you have to talk to them, to ghosts, forcefully, to put them in their place.

I could have also brought Piggy, so he could have at least been my secretary, not left him all messed up like I did, thinking that Piggy wouldn't adjust here, when in reality, the one who didn't adjust was me. I would have brought him with me if, after all, I'd known that the trip would turn out to be free, I had my Makarov for a reason.

Later, Johannes said to me, because they wait until the end to drop the last bomb, that's how they are, women:

"I'm never going to love you, Ricardo, because you're a bad man, I know it, bad. You may fool my father, but you don't fool me, you are a bad man."

"Can't I have changed?"

"I don't think so." She stood up. "Goodbye."

Then she looked directly into my eyes, very seriously, and offered me her hand. I wanted an abyss to open up and the earth to swallow me at that moment, but those things never happen, at least not that quickly, so I shook her hand and asked if I couldn't hold on to the least hope, and why was she saying I was a bad guy when I was just fighting to get ahead like everyone else?

"What you did to Ingrid was very bad."

"Ingrid who?"

"You know very well who, that white chick who studies

dance. You got her pregnant and didn't go with her when she got an abortion, you can't just do that to people."

That bullshit? I thought. Johannes was so naïve.

BERTA

"I don't know anyone in Cabaiguán, I'm not even sure where it is," I told the ghost, and he kept looking at me with his eyes full of tears, and I had to tell him not to worry, that I'd go to this Cabaiguán to see this Araceli and tell her what happened, but, please, stop appearing to me, my nerves were shot enough already.

"Thank you, I know that if you come with me, I'll be able to find the way," he said, and started to become hazier and hazier until he was just a wound and some sad eyes, and thanks to the diazepam, I fell asleep.

I had just turned fourteen, and I'd barely ever left Cienfuegos, much less alone, but the next day when school let out, I went to find out if there was a bus that went to the town of Cabaiguán. The bus terminal was dirty, full of poor people, old people selling everything from newspapers to electric razors, and travelers, and I was expecting at any moment to see the ghost and his rolled-back eyes, so I was hunched over like someone with a fever, and a woman trying to remove a piece of churro from the floor with a broom asked me, "Girl, what's wrong with you?"

"Nothing. What time does the bus for Cabaiguán leave?"

"There has never been a bus from here to that place. But if you wait until tomorrow, you can take a truck that leaves at noon and leaves you right in Cabaiguán itself."

"So how much is it?"

"I don't know, but it can't be much because the little truck is in quite a state."

"Thank you, ma'am."

"You're welcome. I have a daughter your age and I know what that's like."

"What are you talking about?"

"Nothing, you heard me."

"Okay."

I didn't know what I preferred: continuing to see the dead man's face or telling my mother out of nowhere that I needed to go to Cabaiguán and putting up with how much she would surely have to say about the trip. A speech that would surely begin with an emphatic *no* and the declaration that I was strange, really strange. *What are you looking to do in Cabaiguán, you lost something there?* she would say. *To fulfill a promise to a dead man*, I'd have to respond, and my mother would find it in her to send me back to the adolescents' clinic, and everyone in the neighborhood would think I was even crazier than they already did. So I needed to travel without my mother knowing and come back as soon as possible. Later I would say I had slept over at one of so many aunts', cousins', or friends' houses.

"Sir, do you know if the truck that goes to Cabaiguán already came?" I asked an employee.

"Yes, it came already," the man said to me, looking at me like I owed him something.

"How much does it cost?"

"To Cabaiguán itself?"

"Yes."

"Forty pesos."

It was all I had, and that was because I'd sold a Joaquín Sabina MP3 file to the only person in that whole place who liked him, Johannes Stuart.

Well, Aramís, your bad luck, I thought, and went toward the Boulevard. *I can't do anything else. Stealing isn't part of my plan. If you keep showing up, I'll have to get used to it—like menstruation.* My mom wasn't home. That time, one in the afternoon, marks the high point of domino games and all kinds of noise, and I had no desire to go back to our alleyway to face the alcoholics who would undoubtedly harass me: *Berta, you're getting a great body there, man, thin girls with round asses are so pretty. If you cook as well as you walk, I'll eat every last bit.* So I stuck my backpack in a storage locker next to El Encanto, went into the store, and started to look at the clothes and shoes that, according to my mom, we would someday buy ourselves, then I jumped to another store and then another, and when I got to La Mimbre, I saw a naked man sitting right at the entrance, people passed by his side completely untroubled, but I was frozen.

He raised his head and smiled at me. "I thought you'd be in Cabaiguán," he said.

"I didn't have enough money."

"Play number eight, but it has to be early, before the bookies close."

"How much should I play?"

"Ah, I don't know, that's up to you."

"*Padrino*, there's someone who wants to meet you."

"Tell him to come in and you come in, too," he said to me. "Don't forget to pay your respects to the altar."

"Yes, *Padrino*."

"Can I pay my respects, too?" Prince asked.

"Of course, pay your respects."

"Thank you."

"I know him from somewhere."

"Of course, *Padrino*, he's the Stuarts' youngest son."

"Oh, really? They say he's a very good speaker."

"You have to hear him, *Padrino*, he sounds like a president."

"So what's he doing here?"

"He wants to have a talk with you."

"For?"

"To learn, *Padrino*. He's tired of his father's nonsense, Jehovah this, Jehovah that, as if there was nothing else to do."

"Is that true, kid?"

"Yes, sir, it's true."

"Well, well. What about the cathedral? That's quite a building your people are erecting, when it could be that, well, in the worst-case scenario, they wouldn't even let you in, for being black, the Poder Popular people or the Ministry of Education could come along any minute and use it as a school, you'll see. But you can tell you're loaded, that you have ties abroad. I'm the same, I have godchildren in Sweden, Denmark, France, Canada, the U.S.; even in Japan, I have a godson, Koizumi, who, every year, brings me tea and ceramics, all those decorations, he's brought them to me little by little . . . Am I boring you?"

"No, sir, of course not."

"Then pay your respects to the altar and come, sit down; you, Gringo, over in that chair; the kid here, close to me, I want to take a good look at him. How handsome he is, and you can tell he's intelligent. These are the kinds of relationships that are in your best interest, Gringo, not that Salvador whom they call Piggy, that one's not worth a halfpenny. You have to find people who will add something, not take things away from you, my son, pay attention to what I'm saying."

"Yes, *Padrino*, but here, the young man came . . ."

"Yes, I know what he came for, actually, I knew he would come."

PART
TWO

I should have played the whole forty pesos, but my mother says my biggest problem is indecision, and she's absolutely right. I only played twenty pesos. I was about to place them with Chulo, the bookie who lives in *la cuartería*, but I was afraid he would cheat me, so I went to One-Armed Cacha's house and knocked. The one who came to the door was her husband, an old guy who thinks he's good-looking.

"What's this beautiful girl here for?"

"To speak with Cacha."

"Cacha, it's for you," the guy shouted, and One-Armed Cacha showed up, dragging her flip-flops.

"Come in and sit down, my child, you're not going to get any taller just standing there. Did you think about what I said to you?"

"Yes, Cacha, but I'm not interested."

"Okay, but you're missing out . . . with that body you have and that innocent face, you'd have the *yumas* slobbering after you."

"Cacha, I came to bet on a number."

"Now you're into gambling. That's good, let's see if you get ahead at all . . . It makes me sad to see what a hard time you and your mother are going through, just because you feel like it. I already told you what you have to do."

"Leave the girl alone, Cacha," said the guy, who had sat down on one of the rocking chairs in the living room and was looking at me from there. "She must know what she's doing. Right, sweetie?"

"Cacha, I'd like to place twenty pesos on eight."

"Eight, the number of the insignificant dead? That number's not going to come up, better to place it on twenty-four, it's about to come up, I'm telling you, it has been coming close for days."

"No, Cacha, it has to be eight."

"Oh, really? Did you have a dream, perhaps? A revelation?"

"It's not for me, it's a favor I'm doing."

"It's for your mother, isn't it? She's probably drinking again, no one escapes her fate."

"It's for Aramís."

"And who the fuck is that? Your boyfriend?"

"A friend."

"Be careful about the friends you get mixed up with, he could be undercover and I could be getting into a mess."

"No, Cacha, he's a kid from school who's like a brother to me."

"Is he white?"

"Yes."

"Well, well, turns out she has a thing for whites. That's what's with you, that's why you don't want to take up with foreigners. But whites, my child, they, well, the ones here aren't exactly clean."

"Whatever you say, Cacha, but I'm in a bit of a hurry . . . I have to go study."

"'I have to go study.' What's this 'I have to go study,' that doesn't get you anywhere. Give me the money."

GRINGO

"Did you see how easy that was, without a whole lot of talk, without so much bullshit."

"It's true, Ricardo."

"I told you that you'd love him, *Padrino* is the best."

PABLO ARGÜELLES LARA, *the* Padrino

Gringo brought him to me, yes, but when I'd tossed the cowrie shells, Zarabanda Siete Rayos had already told me he was coming and that I should be careful, that I should watch him closely, that I shouldn't let myself be taken in by appearances. Yes, he was a handsome kid. Yes, he had skin that was without a blemish, without a mark, as if he were brand-new. I didn't say much to him, I didn't talk to him about his future, nor did I say this or that, nor that I was going to toss cowrie shells for him, or anything, nor did I give him advice. Who am I to say anything to one who comes to learn but nonetheless looks at me as if he already knows everything, as if he were doing you the favor of visiting you so you would believe certain things and later put on a plaque SAMUEL PRINCE STUART WAS HERE ONE VERY HOT AFTERNOON?

That kid's no good, I thought when he left. *Gringo isn't, either, but he's nothing compared to the other one, together they make a fearsome pair.*

I was looking for a way to make my name, so I went over to see Ordóñez, who had just gotten out of prison, and I started beating on his door. "Who the hell is it?" came a thick voice from inside. The door screeched when it opened, and Ordóñez's wife stuck out first her head full of curlers, then her body, half-covered with a worn robe, and she looked at me with hate in her eyes.

"What's wrong with you?" she said.

I looked her up and down because she was hot, and her cleavage and almost an entire thigh were on display. "Is Ordóñez in?"

"Ordóñez, some kid is looking for you."

I thought, *A kid, hell, you've got so much more than that in store. Start getting your body ready because you're going to end up a widow and the only thing you know how to do is fuck.*

In addition to everything else, I'd had it in for Ordóñez for a while. He was involved in the death of my cousin Luis; he didn't kill him, but he was drinking at the table when Luis was stabbed, everyone said so: *Ordóñez is a good-for-nothing*, but they were scared of him. I wasn't scared of him, I was going to introduce him to his maker.

"Come out," I said to him when he peered out with his fat face. "Look for something with a sharp edge and come out."

"For?" he said, playing dumb.

"You know."

"I don't have to go anywhere."

"Ordóñez, what's this goon's problem with you?" his wife asked. "You just got out of the clink, don't get yourself into trouble, Ordóñez, because this time I'm not going to bring you whatever you need in there. Ordóñez, pay him whatever you owe him. Ordóñez, look, if it's a lot, just give him something to start."

"I don't owe anyone anything."

"Yes, you do owe me," I said. "Luis is dead."

"But I didn't kill him."

"But you were there."

"So what does that have to do with anything? Listen, kid, please, get going, I just got out and I want to lay low, don't fuck up my life."

"Yeah, Guts, please, go on with your life, *muchachito*," she said. "Look, come in, have some orange juice to cool off, listen, I've known you my whole life."

"I don't want some refreshment, I don't want anything, what I want is for this sewer rat to get a knife and come with me."

BERTA

The next day, Cacha came to see me. "Your number won," she says, and gives me the money wrapped up in newspaper. "Buy yourself some clothes," she says. I don't tell her that it's for going to Cabaiguán to fulfill a promise to a dead man; I thank her and ask her not to tell anyone, especially my mother, because she'll start a fight and I'm not up for that.

"Ay, child, who am I going to tell? You do whatever you want with your life, you offend me."

"I'm sorry, Cacha."

"Play another number. Take advantage of the streak, that won't happen again."

"Thank you, but my mother will kill me if she finds out."

It was two thousand pesos, the largest amount of money I'd seen in my life, so I hid a thousand five hundred under the mattress, put the rest away in my backpack, and the following morning left for school. "See you this afternoon," I said to my mother, and gave her a kiss.

"Why are you being so affectionate?"

"No reason, *mamá*."

GRINGO

"Now there's a black president," that's what Billy Holden told me with an ear-to-ear smile, assuming I'd be so happy. He told me yesterday, when he brought my food. "Listen, one of our guys is the president of America."

"How nice." I nodded, although at heart, what did I care, he was not going to pardon me no matter how black he was. When they tell him what I did, he might even move up the execution, so it's all the same to me.

Piggy, if he were here, would sure be happy. Piggy is still as gullible as ever. I'm not gullible anymore; a black president, so what, who cares?

BERTA

Arriving in a town you thought was really small and finding it to be big instead, full of cement-roof houses, *guajiros* on motorcycles flying by with smoke coming out of their exhaust pipes, and *guajiras* who think they are all that, looking first down their noses at your Chinese Mary Janes and then at their own Adidas shoes and thinking you're worse off. Arriving at that town after four hours' journey on a truck overflowing with people and with barely any windows, and asking, "Listen, do you by any chance know an Araceli?"

"No, I don't know her," some said to me.

"Araceli? Araceli what?" a woman, somewhat older, finally said to me as she walked around with a thermos, selling coffee.

"I don't know her last name. I came from Cienfuegos looking for her."

"So what does she sell?"

"As far as I know, nothing."

"So, if you don't know her last name, and she doesn't sell anything, you'd better run home to Cienfuegos, and when you have more information, come back."

"No, I can't come back here; if I leave, I won't return."

"Well, you would know. Do you want some coffee?"

"No, I don't drink coffee."

"Drink it, it will do you good."

"Thank you . . . The Araceli I'm talking about is the girl-friend or wife of an Aramís."

"I know an Aramís."

"What does he look like?"

"He's very white, with black hair."

"That must be him."

"I do know that Aramís, and his father and his brothers . . . Are you with him?"

"No, ma'am, it's something else."

"Then he's with your sister, because he sold a load of oxen and went to Cienfuegos under the pretext of buying a motor-cycle and he never came back . . . If he didn't go to the *Yuma*, he must be there with some *mulata*, because he always fell for the darker girls."

"I came with a message of his that I have to give to that Araceli. Try to remember, please, there has to be some Araceli."

"Araceli? Araceli? . . . The only Araceli I know is Ferreiro's wife, and I don't know what message you could give her on behalf of Aramís Ramírez . . . I mean, as far as I know, Ferreiro and Aramís have never gotten along."

"So where can I find her?"

"Well, what's the message?"

"That doesn't matter."

"So tell me."

"He asked me not to tell anyone."

"You're pretty mysterious for being so young."

"What can you do? We're like that in Cienfuegos."

"Cienfuegos is shit. Santa Clara is better."

"Whatever you say. Where does that Araceli live?"

"Continue along this street and turn to the right, she's at the second house . . . I think the door is painted blue."

"Thank you."

"You're welcome. Be careful, guys around here go crazy for *mulatas* . . . since there aren't many."

ARAMÍS

Nothing they say about death is enough, it consumes you by the second, when you least expect it, you're already in it, you begin to realize it when everything becomes relative, removed from you, cold and distant, just like it sounds, cold and distant. I'm already dead, which is a way of saying that I'm already on the other side of the wall, with just one small opening to see life, and that window is you, Berta, my window; through it, I can see myself arriving in Cienfuegos in search of a motorcycle, I see the feverish face of the man who killed me, and I see the liquid that will kill him, entering his veins, and then I realize that revenge is useless, it's nothing but an advance against the final payment, and I'm fine with having already left behind my body of a young man, all muscle, my face that was envied by men and loved by women, I'm happy to have gone, Berta, happy; nevertheless, nevertheless, is she there? Tell me if she's there, Berta? And if she's there, tell her I can't forget her, that I try and that sadness over not having been worthy of her prevents me from rising, going up to whatever regions I'd most like. Tell her, Berta, tell her: *Araceli, Aramís is here next to me, he's dead, but it's as if he were alive because he thinks of you with the same pain as always, and he'd like to say more to you, he'd like to tell you about the great beyond, about death, but that's forbidden, it's closed off behind that door with seven seals, and he's forced into silence, but if it weren't like that, he would speak.* Tell her, Berta, tell her. How is she? She looks pretty.

Yes, she's wearing white and some really beautiful sandals.

Tell her then, go to my father's house, and beneath the plum tree beside the door, there's a crate buried with twelve golden rings; tell her to give one to you and take the rest for herself, and then she can leave that idiot husband of hers, she's too pretty for him; tell her, Berta, tell her.

She's not going to believe me.

Tell her.

Fine.

"What did you say?" the blond girl asked.

"He says to go to his father's house, and there beneath the plum tree . . ."

"Ask him who killed him."

"He says that's not important, that you should go to the plum tree . . ."

"Get out of my house," the blond girl said and stood up. "Out."

GRINGO

They're going to kill me, just like it sounds, they're going to inject me with some kind of mixture so that I go to sleep and never wake up; and sitting before me, behind glass, will be the families of the Americans I bumped off, they'll be looking at me, watching how I die little by little: *It's showtime*. They're going to kill me, at least that's what they think, but maybe I'll turn into an insect or a small bird, I'll turn into a *zunzún*, a bee hummingbird, and I'll escape through the window before they inject the first fluid, which is the one that hurts, the one that puts you to sleep, at least that's what my fat black guard says, who also says that if he had a face like mine, he never would have spent his time killing women, instead he would be happily enjoying life, but unfortunately, he was born with the face of a damn otter and had to spend his time doing this, taking care of death row prisoners, even though he used to play football before he hurt his knee. You would be good as a politician, as governor, I say to him, now that there's a black president, maybe they'll appoint you. But he says, nah, he says, politicians tell a lot of lies and I'm not up for that, all I want is to pay my taxes and for Teresa to love me. Teresa is his wife, a fat black woman with a kind face, who sometimes sends me pancakes and a piece of roast that looks like plastic. "If I'd met someone like Teresa when I was still in Cuba, things wouldn't have become so twisted," I say sometimes, fooling myself, but since I was fourteen years old, I've only known bad whores, hypocrites, and prisses like that Johannes, that she-devil.

ROGELIO

A temple, something that, in these times when everything is in decline, dares to rise up and say, *I'm here despite it all, I'm here, look at me.*

GUTS

I was going to end him. When I called him outside, it was to end him and let disgrace catch up with me, immerse myself in disgrace and being a born fuckup, but he didn't come out, he didn't grab a knife or do anything like that. I think he even pissed his pants. All he did was look at me from behind his wife's back, and I yelled at him *chicken, maricón,* and everything else that went through my head.

GRINGO

I didn't want to find out what it is that they inject into you, but that fool Billy Holden found out for me and even brought me a printout that describes, with that abundance of detail that Americans seem to love, the advantages of sodium pentothal over other chemical substances also used for lethal injection.

Sodium pentothal, I whispered to myself several times, but it didn't sound like anything to me, it wasn't like saying *a stabbing* or *a machete wound*. That Holden spends his time bodybuilding. He must have the metabolism of a city rat, since he can eat a large bucket of Kentucky Fried Chicken and be hungry again within two hours. With one of those buckets, you can feed a whole block in Cuba and have some left over for the next day. That big black guy is an eating machine and I tell him so.

"If you end up in prison, your ass is theirs," I tell him, and he laughs because he has biceps that look more like a fat woman's thighs and he thinks that makes him a tough guy. He's wrong. Piggy was also strong and didn't have any courage; he bragged, but at heart he was just a little bunny, so after the pigs left, I went to get him and said to him:

"Piggy, we've got to get the hell out of here. But they're watching me and the trip by boat to the *Yuma* is at least ten thousand dollars a head. So you know the deal, go to La Mimbre and knock off a *guajiro*, but one who has money. Go, I'll wait for you here."

"I don't have it in me to do that."

"Oh, really? What in the fuck do you have it in you to do, Piggy, if I may ask?"

"The other thing, selling meat."

"Well, look, you're going to have to find it in you because we can't go on, they're already after us."

"What kind of mess have you gotten me into?" Piggy looked at me with fearful eyes, then he told me he didn't want to go to the *Yuma*, that his mother was old and who was going to take care of her, and besides, the cold made him break out in hives.

"You're going to break out in hives when they execute you. The AKM rips huge holes in your chest, the size of a fist, and then they bury you in one of those checked shirts we all have so no one can see the big holes."

"But I didn't kill anyone," Piggy insisted.

"The one who kills the cow is as guilty as the one who holds it down," I said to him, and he shook his head again, and I thought, *I'm going to bump off this filthy pig before he rats on me, I'm going to finish him off, and then I'm going to sell his meat to the same dumbasses in Punta Gorda who feed off* guajiros.

"Piggy, I'll be waiting for you at Tita's house at ten in the morning, that's where we're going to see this through, so don't fail me."

"But what if I can't find a *guajiro*?"

"Get one, tell him they're selling a 1959 Chevy with a diesel engine."

GUTS

I was going to end him. When I said, "Come out," it was to end him, but something saved him, I thought at the time. *Something saved me*, I think now. I would be in jail right now with Nacho Fat-Lips and Gordo Gris, looking at each other's faces, waiting to see who ended who first, and not here in Barcelona, eating out white girls I have to call *usted*, white girls with thighs, not skinny or long legged. I went on with life thanks to that degenerate disappointing me. *This old lady's an ex-con? This old hag is a kingpin?* I thought, when I saw how scared he was of what a kid like me could do to him, me, only

85

sixteen then. Now, here in Barcelona, the ruffians pass right by me and I don't pay them any mind, although one day at the entrance to the metro, some asshole said to me in Catalan, "Down with blacks," he yelled it in my face. I still remember his green hair and his leather jacket. There were three of them, but only the most brutish one spoke, the other two looked somewhat embarrassed. "This fucking Arab doesn't understand when I speak a Christian language," he told his friends when I didn't respond, since he was going for the jugular. I was working as a bouncer at a club in the city and it wasn't in my best interest to dirty my uniform, so I sighed and tried to let it go, but the one with the green hair called me Arab again and black monkey, he got close to me and breathed in my face, and that's one thing I cannot stand; when someone comes for me, I'll meet them there. I threw myself at all three of them. It was as if I'd gone back to Cienfuegos. I hit them hard and then I took my dick out and pissed on the green-haired one's face, it meant shit to me if he was Catalan and we were in fucking Barcelona, if you come for me, I'm there. "These blacks should be deported," a woman said behind me, but I'm a Spanish citizen, I've got my papers in order and I'm married to Jimena, who is Catalan, and my father-in-law is so cheap that you have to ask his permission to so much as eat an apple.

BERTA

If I didn't go mad then, I can be assured that I won't ever go mad, because when that girl with her martyr's face announcing *mylifeissohard* asked me to leave her house, the dead man literally grabbed me by the arm and there is nothing worse than being touched by the dead. When an ectoplasm touches you with its cold fingers, you don't feel it on your arm: you feel it in your very heart, you feel as if it has stopped beating and you're frozen, just dangling there.

Tell her I'm here, Aramís pressed.

I already told her, I said.

Tell her again, tell her I miss her, tell her to believe you and not to worry, that her husband just went to Javier's house and they just took out a bottle of rum and he's going to be a while.

I repeated it all to the blond girl.

She asked me, "What brand is the rum?"

Havana Club, seven years, the dead man said.

"Havana Club, seven years," I said.

She started crying because it was true, her husband only drank Havana Club. "Tell him to tell you who killed him, ask him." She fell into a chair again, close to a print of the Sacred Heart of Jesus looking down on us sweetly.

Tell her that doesn't matter, the dead man said, *tell her that would only serve to worry her, and for me, time no longer exists and now I see a lethal injection entering my murderer's veins and how he writhes around.*

"Ask him how I'm going to die," she said. "Ask him how long I have left of this martyrdom, how long I will have to put up with this animal."

Tell her not to be afraid, he said, *to go where I said and get the gold, and to give you one and then escape together.*

Together with me? Why me?

It's a manner of speaking, the dead man said, *although I'd like for the two of you to stay together, Araceli likes poetry just like you do.*

Yeah, but I have my own life, I have my mother, I'm from Cienfuegos.

And you live in a neighborhood where you'll probably get killed and maybe even raped first.

GRINGO

I had a big cast-iron pot where I boiled the heads until they lost all traces of meat and skin. Then with a hammer, I cracked the skulls into pieces and asked my *Padrino*'s permission to put them in the Nganga. I also took a phalange from the fingers of each dead person and two bits from the ankles. I had a special use reserved for Piggy's skull. Salvador Piggy was going to work for me. I was going to own his head, there's nothing better than a cowardly dead man like him, a dead *pendejo* that tells you about everything in advance. So I sharpened my knife and waited for him, I was sure he would come alone, but to my surprise, he came with someone. A woman, a *guajira*.

"Look what I brought you, Gringo," he said, euphoric, peering in with that passing-for-white black man's face of his. "This young lady wants an air-conditioning unit, she brought the money and everything."

I looked at her. She was pretty young, but she was fat. In fact, she looked swollen, her face even looked like that of a diabetic.

Could she be a cop? I thought, because it didn't even pass through my mind that Piggy would be capable of sweet-talking a girl and bringing her here, even a girl like this one, who screamed *guajira* with those bloodred boots that, in the light, looked like they were real leather.

"How's the young lady doing?" I said, and held out my hand.

"So-so," she said.

"Listen, don't be shy," Piggy said, "this is my buddy, talking to him is like talking to me."

Then, with that naïve, obstinate way that Cuban women have, she closed the small distance between us and gave me a kiss on the cheek. *Poor thing*, I thought, if I didn't need the money so much to get out of there, I'd have let her go, but I needed the dough, and Piggy, the other candidate in the running, didn't have a dime in his pockets, so the perfect candidate to be a corpse was her, there was no way around it.

"Take a seat, don't be shy; you, too, *tarugo*, you're not going to get any taller just standing there. What's your name, sweetheart?"

"Amarilis."

"What a pretty name . . . I'm Ricardo Mora, at your service."

"I know you from somewhere. Are you by any chance an artist?"

"This guy doesn't even sing in the shower," fucking Piggy butted in.

"No, my dear, I studied civil engineering and I work to be of service to pretty girls like you."

"Engineer, how fancy." She seemed to relax. She even uncrossed her legs.

"What do you do?"

"Oh, I'm a housewife. My husband grows tobacco, in Chambas."

"Chambas, Ciego de Ávila," Piggy said euphorically, and

opened his eyes so wide they looked like they were going to pop out.

"Of course," I said. "Chambas, Ciego de Ávila, it wouldn't be Chambas, Piggy's Backside."

"You're so funny!" She looked at me with her brown, fat-girl's eyes. She wouldn't be half-bad if you took off those hip-high pants and the too-tight blouse that didn't suit her body at all.

"Do you want a beer?" I asked her. "*Tarugo*, open the fridge and take out a lager for each of us."

"So you're selling an air conditioner," she said. "One of the big ones?"

"Enormous. LG with a remote control and everything."

"Is it white?"

"Like a coconut."

"So how much are you asking?"

"Well, this one cost me seven hundred CUC, I can't give it to you for less than six-fifty."

BERTA

He said, *Come on, Berta, go look for the gold, don't take any longer 'cause the guy is about to come back, tell Araceli not to pack anything, that there are better clothes for sale in Cienfuegos anyway.*

"But I can't leave just like that, *imaginate*, I have to talk to my husband first. I'm sure that if I leave, he'll call the police, and they'd be willing to go look for me and bring me back, you don't know what the *guajiros* around here are like."

Leave him a note, the dead man told me to say to her, and I said so and she looked for a pencil and paper.

"What do I write?" she asked.

"Write anything," I said, but Aramís said, *Write: I don't love you anymore, Alcibíades Ferreiro, it's over between us because you are too violent a man for me and you will never understand a sensitive woman like me, who loves art and poetry. Goodbye, Alcibíades, don't look for me.*

"If I write that down, he'll go out looking for me with a machete, and then there will be one more person dead." She put the pencil on the table and burst out crying.

There's no time to cry, the dead man said, *do what I tell you, he's not going to look for you because he is in love with Elisa.*

I told her.

"Elisa, that whore?" she said, but then she got angry and picked up the pencil again.

Once she finished the letter, the girl took the notebook with her best poems, her newest bras and underwear, a brand-new pair of jeans, and the picture of her recently deceased mother and put it all in a backpack.

"Wait for me here," she said; she went to the house next door, asked to borrow a shovel and spade, and we went to look for the gold.

It was where the dead man had told us it would be, a crate inside which was an old canvas bag with twelve gold rings.

We took a taxi to Cienfuegos and became friends on the way. We had so many things in common that it was incredible. She had just turned seventeen, which made her much older than me; nonetheless, compared to me, she was like a little girl. She held the backpack where we had put the gold on her lap, and I would say to her, "Relax, Araceli, relax."

"Aren't you Ferreiro's wife?" the driver had asked when we

got to the house, in front of which was one of those Cubataxis that only accepts CUCs.

"I left him."

"Ferreiro's going to kill you."

"Ferreiro's a dumbass," Araceli said, still worked up and full of anger. "If you see him, tell him that I said to take Elisa to the house. From now on, she'll be the one who washes the clothes and tends to the goddamn ulcer on that goddamn foot on that shitty diabetic who doesn't take care of himself!"

"I'll tell him," the taxi driver said with a sigh, then scratched the part of his chest peeking out of his open shirt. "So who's this?"

"My lover," Araceli said, and the taxi driver got very serious and said he wasn't on the clock and couldn't take us, and he was sorry but he'd have to tell Ferreiro.

"How much to Cienfuegos?" Araceli then asked.

"It's fifty dollars, but if you give me a hundred CUC over that, I'll leave you right at the door of the house, and if it's a hotel, I'll take you one by one up to the room and sing you a wedding march."

"That's not necessary." She took out the money, along with an extra ten dollars that she gave to the driver so he would keep his mouth shut.

ROGELIO

Someone started to say it one day, and by the time we tried to stop it, it was too late. The rumor was growing even more quickly than the building, it got away from us. The situation became favorable for us; suddenly from all over Cuba the donations poured in, and we were able to install marble instead of the granite I'd planned on. In addition, the bureaucratic machine turned strangely permissive and gave us one permit after another as if it had decided, just like that, on benevolence toward the congregation of the Holy Sacrament. Arturo was of the opinion that it was simply God's influence that was on our side, but I always knew it was something else, and one day my wife confirmed it for me. "Everyone is saying," she said, "that in Cienfuegos they're building the Black Cathedral." I was struck dumb, listening to her. I had to sit down. She poured me a glass of water, and then I understood why so many had become understanding, and even helpful, why that multitude of neighbors was working with us, why the temple itself seemed to overflow, to make itself larger, to the point that it seemed like a schizophrenic building; why I myself put aside what was planned, chalking it up to the influx of money, so where there was once a sixteen-foot gap between columns, I now tried to make it twice as big. I understood it all. I understood that the temple was cursed, corrupt, that it was a praise song not just to the very concept of people with a lot of melanin in their skin, but that it was called the Black Cathedral for those with darkness in their hearts, and nothing could dissuade me from that idea. So I made the final modifications to dozens of plans and I went to see Arturo Stuart. "This is as far as I go," I told him, and handed over the sketches. "Find someone else," I told him. His whole family was there, Johannes was sitting at the living room table sketching a horse, and the mother and the two boys were watching television. Arturo Stuart didn't flinch. "Do you want more money?" he asked right there, in front of his family, as if I were a damn salesman.

"It's not the money."

"Then what?"

It seemed so irrational to declare that the temple was cursed, that we were erecting the cathedral of evil, that it was a cursed angel who had suggested its shape in my dreams, that I had to tell him:

"I have my reasons, but I prefer not to make them known; ultimately, you no longer need an architect as much as a civil engineer, someone who can bring a comprehensive end to the mad factory that's now come of the temple we once saw as restrained, rational, practically a return to the principles of Le Corbusier . . . But, unfortunately, the temple is sick, and I don't have the medicine to cure it, nor am I a Gaudí to go on with this madness, I have to save myself.

"I have to save myself," I repeated, and now it all seems a little crazy. When you resolve to say what you're thinking, you say things that leave you in shock; my only way to achieve renown, to be remembered, I now understand, was that building, and I threw it away, I gave it up like it didn't matter to me.

I was kind of crazy then, I understand, too many sleepless nights, too much coffee, too many demands, and even too much money, for a building that grew, that overflowed, that half-finished was larger even than the Catholic cathedral of Cienfuegos, the one that seemed to regard us with mistrust from Martí Park.

IBRAHIM

The temple began like an airplane taking off, to become an ally of the air, master of the winds. "We're making a book, this is a book in stone," Arturo Stuart would say to us, and you looked into his eyes and could believe what he was saying because we really were building a sacred book. The cathedral was growing and, with it, our longing to love, to follow the example of real Christians, we were creating the temple of end times, the New Jerusalem was now beginning to rise up in Cienfuegos, we felt that nothing could stop us, we sang on our way to work, we the humble ceased to be humble, and nothing could stop us. "We're making a book," Arturo Stuart said to us, and he spoke to us of Gothic cathedrals erected in the time of Catholicism, that were actually songs to God, he spoke to us about our church being something like that, a true song to God, and when he said so, we all stood up in praise.

"This temple has no head or tail," my wife said to me when I told her about it. "You can't begin to fry a fish and, half-way through your meal, pray for it to become chicken. Fish or chicken? One or the other . . . At the beginning, they started with something modest, so that the congregation would have somewhere to meet, and now it's not like that, now they want to amaze Cienfuegos, and with this city, the world. The authorities won't allow it, you can bet on that."

My wife is a woman of little faith, I've been married to her for twenty years and she's my cross to bear, I haven't managed to make her settle her affairs with Christ, I respect her because she's the mother of my children and she is concerned for me, but she should be careful about what she says.

"Look at how skinny you are," she continued. "You've spent nearly six years tangled up in the building of that church, it's not like it's a volunteer microbrigade and we're going to get our own house in return for your work; there's no oil for cooking here, there's nothing, Elsa has no shoes, I'm sending her to school in her dress-up sandals and I can't take it anymore . . . I curse the day that you dedicated yourself to Jehovah."

"Yahweh," I told her, because Yahweh is the true name of God, and I took it as a teaching moment. "One day, you'll get close to Christ and then you'll see that every sacrifice was worth it, that nothing was in vain, that day will come."

"Why didn't you devote yourself to the lottery?" she said. "It would have been better for you to run numbers, then we wouldn't be wanting for anything in this house. I don't know what I'm going to do, really, I don't know, they're going to make cuts to our staff and since I'm the newest one there, I'm practically on the street, and, well . . . Tell Stuart to give you something, to pay you. Too many dollars come into that church for you to keep working for free. You working hard and them living like Croesus . . . How long, *Árabe*?"

"Shut up, woman."

GRINGO

When I got to Portland, there were almost no Latinos and even fewer Cubans, so from the beginning they thought I was a black American. I had to start speaking black, not that English whites speak where they put *do* in front of everything. No black man says *Do you want to drink?* like they showed me at school in Miami. They come out with *Yuguandrink?* And that's that, and if you even dream of speaking any other way, they think you're putting on airs, that you're a damn Ph.D., or something like that. The one who got me excited about running out to Portland was my brother. When I met up with him in Little Havana, he took me to his tiny apartment, and after treating me to several beers, a gift of a hundred dollars, and two outfits, he told me he was a pizza-delivery guy and that it was going well for him.

That made me laugh. "You came from so far away to deliver pizzas. No one is going to believe that. I came here to be a winner."

"Well, there's no work, and taxes are killing me, you pay them for everything here."

"So why don't you become a mobster?"

"You've seen too many movies. Here, the law is king. Here, to be a drug trafficker or do anything under the radar, you have to have connections, you don't just wake up and decide to do it. Listen, we're not in Cienfuegos, look out that window and see the skyscrapers. You can't get around by foot here; if you don't have a car, you're screwed like you can't believe, *imagínate* . . . Mobster? Don't make me laugh."

"Well, I came here to get ahead, if I wanted to be some nobody going from house to house, I would've stayed in Cuba."

From her chair, my brother's wife—a little *mulata* with an oriental face who later turned out to be Salvadoran—gave me a crazed look, anxious for me to leave and stop corrupting her man.

"So how's everyone from the neighborhood?" he asked me.

"How do you think? Same as always, you can imagine," I said to him, and took a long sip. "The last one I saw was Piggy, he wanted to come, but he started drinking and lost part of the dough at el Ruso's bar with a new whore, a Yusimí."

"Yusimí Cabrera?"

"I don't know, Yusimí something."

"A *mora* with green eyes?"

"That's the one."

"Well, well. Salvador is still a drag, but maybe it's better that he stayed there. You've got to work a lot here and not leave anything to the state, it's not like Cuba here."

"It's worse here," I told him. "In Hialeah, some Puerto Ricans came up to me to sell me drugs."

"It's the clothes you're wearing," my brother said with a disapproving stare. "You've spent nearly all the money you brought from Cuba on looking fancy. Besides, those *boricuas* have connections, you don't do anything here without connections."

"How am I supposed to get ahead looking like shit?" I asked my brother, and looked at the Salvadoran woman, who, although her body wasn't much, wasn't all that ugly. "I could've stayed in Cuba if I was going to keep wearing cheap little shirts."

"You're not cut out for Miami; Chicago, New York, or something like that is more your thing," my brother said, and I took another drink, and he talked to me about Portland, he told me he had gone on vacation there and liked it, but he was allergic to the flowers, besides, it got cold there, an arctic cold, the kind that chaps your ears, and the sky was gray, and you had to go around wearing a mountain of clothes not to freeze.

"The blacks that live there are starting to get pale," he said, "and when they go to Cuba, they almost pass for white."

"But there is a lot of work to be found there," the Salvadoran woman butted in, and I told both of them I'd think about it.

"Take advantage while it's summer," he said, and then I told him that, yes, I was going to fly on a plane for the first time in my life, and within a month I was first in Seattle, then in Portland.

In Portland, I met my first American lady. Her name was Elsa Pound and she had diabetes, so she went to the grocery stores to buy sugar-free cookies and Diet Coke. She saw me at one of these stores when I was about to return to Miami, and it was as if she bought me. She talked to me and I understood her quite well because she spoke a very correct English, like in the movies. I already had experience working on women like that, self-important fat women with college degrees: in Cuba, I'd had a fortysomething who worked at the Housing Department and thought she was so great because she could take any poor sap's house away from him. I fucked her any which way as long as I could stay at her apartment and get out of the neighborhood for a while, since the police were looking for me back then for the "illegal sacrifice of major livestock," as they call it.

Speaking of livestock, my first dead man, Aramís, came to see me on my *Padrino*'s behalf, since he remains in the Nganga working for him, and although he's an enslaved dead man, he thinks he's all that. I thought it was somewhat amusing. I said to him, "*Guajiro*, want me to sell you a motorbike?" And he didn't say anything, he smiled to himself, since he knows I'll soon be dead, too. "But at least no one's going to stick me in anyone's pot," I said to him. The other one, the one who wanted the plasma TV, that one hasn't come to see me, I can tell my *Padrino* wants him for some special job. The one who screwed me up was the dead woman I brought from Cuba, I shouldn't have listened to Piggy, I should have let the little fat woman go, but she was so anxious to buy her air conditioner that when I started to pull back and to offer buts—*Maybe this won't work out because those units turn out badly and you've got to give me the money right now, and besides, I don't offer any kind of guarantee*—she got up from the chair, took me first by the arm, then opened her purse and showed me her money.

"Look, it's all here," she said.

No one can just show me that much money, as if I were a meek little dove, I thought once I'd slit her throat. She drowned in her own blood right away and fell like a baby chick. She had skin as smooth as if it were brand-new. You could tell that *guajira* bathed with special soaps and then slathered creams all over herself. She smelled good, a light fragrance, nothing overpowering. Piggy helped me undress her, looking at her with hungry eyes, thinking I would let him fuck her, but I said to him, "None of that, to fuck you've got to do the job well, and who the fuck told you to bring a woman, huh, goddammit, Piggy?"

"But you killed her."

"I didn't have any choice." Then I noticed that I'd gotten hard looking at the dead woman, her fat woman's skin, fat woman's rolls. I could never love one of those white women, one of those fat women, my ideal was Johannes, an athletic black woman, proud as a princess, but Johannes didn't love me, and this Amarilis had something about her. So I told Piggy to go get the instruments. When I was left alone, I took a rag and cleaned the blood off the *guajira* and then I fucked her. I shouldn't have done it: it's one thing for someone to kill you and sell you as food out of necessity, and another for them to also abuse your mortal remains. "Take your time," I'd said to Piggy, and when he returned, I was already turning her into little fillets.

That dead woman ruined me, I should never have brought anything of hers up North, I should have given her to my *Padrino* or left her in peace in Cienfuegos, but back then, I didn't know about how the dead long for revenge, I thought they were just slaves.

Piggy saved himself big-time because I was going to snuff him out, not because I had anything against him, but so as not to leave any loose ends. Piggy would have been a useful dead man, principled, noble, he would have warned me, he would have told me not to stop in Dalhart, and I wouldn't have gone down like such a dumbass, that afternoon that they caught me. *Texas, the state of the brave.* Texas can go to hell with its grass, its horses, its brave men, along with this whole country and its black president.

GUTS

Sometimes I take to wandering Las Ramblas, and without realizing it I go for blocks and blocks, and when I stop, I find that I've gotten far from my house, then I sit down in a small bar called Monserrate and I ask for a Cuba Libre, which never tastes the same as the ones in Cienfuegos. The owner of the bar is Chilean, his name is Agustín and he admires General Pinochet; when he gets to talking about that, I tell him to be quiet. *Cubano*, he says to me, *what you guys need is a Pinocchio to make you shape up*. I don't say anything, I stick to watching him and think that at another time I would have crossed the bar to slap him across the face for being fresh, because I was like that, always looking for someone to rough up. Sometimes I remember the Stuart brothers, and get a load of this, I think I would have liked to get to know Prince better, maybe we would have gotten along, but over there, you have fixed ideas, you think things can only be a certain way, and when they're not, you get scared.

That Prince, after Gringo took off up North, got into literature, it was the strangest thing in the world, suddenly, he became a poet or wanted to become a poet, because when you're born for something, you can't escape your fate, and he was born to be bad, to be wicked. Bertica, Araceli, and he went together to a literary workshop run by some hairy dude who sometimes stopped by el Ruso's bar to have a few drinks and see those nymphos shake their tits back and forth. I know because el Ruso, otherwise known as Antón Abramovich, was the one who gave me a job when I got kicked out of my house for not going to school or working. I was staying with Nacho Fat-Lips, my imprisoned brother, and I went right to Abramovich's office and asked him for a job, and he told me no problem, and the next day I started with something easy. Then I made it to collecting bets for dogfights, and I had to break more than a few bones, among them Salvador Piggy's, he owed two thousand pesos. I went to see him in that filthy place he called his room, and when I laid into him with the first hit and threw him to the floor, he told me that if Gringo were there, I wouldn't have the courage to do what I was doing. "I could give a fuck about Gringo," I whispered low to him, and then I kicked him a few times in the ribs, I took out my dick and pissed on his face. Back then, I was solid, I was already six foot two, and even though I was kind of skinny, I was really sinewy, I would have been the tallest in the neighborhood if not for Cricket. Cricket was almost six foot five and had a terrifyingly large cock, everyone in the neighborhood knew it.

El Ruso was looking to expand his business and called me over one day and said, "Listen, Yohandris, I want to put together a porno show for tourists. I already have the girls, but I need a guy who looks good, is tall, and who has a really big one."

"A really big one?"

"Yeah, he has to be well-endowed, truly well-endowed." El Ruso made an eloquent gesture.

I went to see Cricket, who, as always, was taking a beating from his father and working on that cathedral that seemed endless, and I said to him, *"Oye, chavo."*

"What's up?"

"You wanna earn some cash? Like real cash."

"What do I have to do? Because if it's cracking skulls, I'm not made for that."

"Don't worry, your part is easy, all you have to do is fuck."

"Fuck? Up the ass? Nah, that's not for me."

"What do you mean up the ass, Cricket? Do I look like a queer to you or what? Fuck some chicks that are really hot, the best kind of whites, blondes, beauties, *mulatas*, your favorite . . . even Yusimí, the black girl with green eyes."

"Yusimí the pretty one? Doesn't she have some kind of kidney disease?"

"She's already been operated on, I think. Besides, what do you care? You should be happy, you're going to get to stop jerking off, you're going to be the most admired guy in this whole shithole, your dick's going to wear out from so much fucking."

"That's a sin."

"Sin, my ass, man. You peep, you jerk off, you rub up against girls on the bus . . . One more sin isn't going to kill you."

"Yes, but those are venial sins, this other thing you're asking me to do is really something, Guts, it's putting the health of my immortal soul in jeopardy."

"The hell with your soul. I don't even have a soul, and look how great things are for me, with the best clothes and a harem of white women after me. You're still at school and getting whatever crumbs you can. How long can you do that, Cricket?"

"Fair enough," he said.

I took him to the bar, and when he saw the girls up close and smelled their perfume that el Ruso had people bring him all the way from Paris and saw how the girls sprayed it on like water, the dumbass nearly lost his mind and the girls noticed, and I think they got a little scared of him, all of them except Yusimí, the black girl with Indian features who really thought she was some kind of panther, because even though she was el Ruso's favorite, she went over and said to Cricket, "Take it out, we want to see it."

GRINGO

I gave him his half and told him, all serious, "Listen, Salvador, I'm going to Sagua to plan the trip. You, keep doing your thing so no one gets suspicious, but don't have a single drink, and if anyone asks about me, tell them I'm on a spiritual retreat because of my Christian faith."

"Okay," Piggy said, "no problem. When are you coming back?"

"Soon."

I got to Havana and went to see my cousin Osiris and told him to find me a contact, the kind with connections to guys running speedboats, since I had an urgent need to leave the country.

"Do you know how much that costs?" Osiris asked. "Ten thousand big ones. Don't tell me you have that much money because I won't believe you."

"I don't, but my brother does."

He told me that he knew an individual who could take me to Mexico, but to not even think of pulling one over on him because those people wouldn't be understanding; I might be someone in Cienfuegos, but I wouldn't be worth as much as a flip-flop to the Mexican Mafia. Okay, I said to him, and right there, I dropped fifty CUC on him for doing me that favor, then I gave him the address of Ana Lidia, my girl from Centro Habana. Three days later, Osiris came to see me.

"Everything's ready, tomorrow at two a.m. you should be at a place on the coast, near Santa María, and try to get there on time because they won't wait for you. They're going to flash their lights twice, then you'll jump in the water and swim over to the cigarette boat. Is that clear?"

"Clear as can be."

"Listen, buddy, the guys on the cigarette boat demand some cash in advance to prove that you're serious and that they won't need to send your pretty fingers to your brother in Miami to release the money, like they've had to do other times."

I gave him two hundred dollars.

"How many are there?" I asked.

"Three, but why are you worried about that?"

"No reason, *primo*, no reason." To reassure him, I added, "I just don't want them to decide to throw me overboard."

"Don't worry, they're serious guys and they're not going to risk their business for ten thousand lousy dollars. Besides, you're lucky, on this trip, you'll be the only passenger, so you'll have the whole cabin to yourself."

"How'd that happen?"

"They didn't explain it to me, but it must be that someone dropped out."

"What luck." I sighed.

"That's right." Osiris asked if I was taking my lady friend with me, since he had taken a look at Ana Lidia at one of her shows at the cabaret, which was precisely where she was at that moment.

"Where the hell am I going to get another ten thousand dollars from?" I said. "If you want, I'll write her a letter from over there telling her all about you."

"No, you'd better not."

When he left, I opened my backpack, took out my gun, unloaded it, cleaned and oiled it, and confirmed that it was in good condition.

Whatever I know about weapons I learned before I dedicated myself to the fast life, when I was in the Special Forces. They also taught me how to use all kinds of sharp weapons:

bayonets, switchblades, sabers, machetes, although my favorite were the knives.

For Ana Lidia, I left fifty dollars on top of the night table and wrote her a letter. I also wrote to Piggy, sending him to hell for being a *pendejo* and recommending that he not say a thing because he was going to screw himself over, and to Prince, to whom, in addition to saying goodbye, I was leaving my motor scooter and everything he could take out of my house before the police came to make their inventory and keep it all.

I closed my backpack, where I only carried a piece of Amarilis's skull, bones from her fingers and toes, three pairs of underwear, a shirt, soap, an electric razor, toothpaste, and a toothbrush.

The gun I put away in my pants, strapping it in with my belt, so it would be easy to grab when needed. The switchblade I put in the sock of my right foot.

I went out to the street, took the bus to the outskirts of the city, and walked to the place Osiris had specified. I got there around twelve at night. I had eaten before I went out and I've never been a big eater, but I was already hungry when, at nearly three in the morning, I saw the blinking of lights in the sea's darkness.

As soon as I got on the speedboat, I figured out that the only opponent of any size was the shortest of the Mexicans; you could tell by the determination in his voice. He asked me if the thing about my brother was true, because, if not, he would throw me in the water right there and not have to do it in the middle of the shark-infested Gulf.

"As true as the fact that I'm going to die one day," I said to him, and only then did he shake my hand, and then the Cuban and the other Mexican also greeted me.

The cigarette boat was manned by the Cuban and it really flew. The guys offered me a beer and put on music, none of this reggaeton or salsa. Real music. Pure symphonic rock is what these fucking guys listened to.

I liked them, actually, but it was them or me. I was sure that my brother wasn't going to send any money to keep me whole, since he most probably didn't have ten thousand dollars, so when one of them, after I told him how girls from Cienfuegos like to fuck, told me we were almost there—"What you see over there are Mérida's lights"—I asked, "Where can I take a piss? This beer has my bladder all swollen."

"The bathroom is downstairs, in the cabin," the other one said to me, the less squat one. "Although if you want, *cuate*, piss in the sea, but be careful not to fall. Even if you drown, your brother is still going to have to pay us the ten thousand dollars."

I entered the bathroom.

I prepared the gun.

First, I shot at the toughest one, who almost got his weapon out, but I got him in the head; the other one was stunned, looking at me, he didn't make the least gesture, I don't know how he decided to start trafficking people since he had no courage. The Cuban one, focused on steering, hadn't heard the shots: the engines were loud, the boat was almost thirty-three feet long, and the deceased men and I were close to the stern.

I came up behind him and shouted to him, "Listen, *compatriota*, the *charros* fell in the water."

"What?" But when he saw the gun, he understood quite clearly; first he thought I was a State Security agent—imagine that, really.

He had to explain to me how to operate the cigarette boat, which is actually simple, like a car, except you have to be careful with the waves. Together, that Cheo and I went along the Mexican coast, leaving behind Mérida, Campeche, Coatzacoalcos.

I ended up killing him when we were parallel to the U.S., near a town I later learned was called Brownsville. I threw him overboard. I had thrown the Aztecs overboard before, after taking the money out of their pockets. I also threw over the gun and the knife, and I cleaned the blood off the deck. I navigated until I was relatively close to the coast. I jumped and went swimming to the shore, leaving the cigarette boat adrift.

I could only butcher enough English to lure in some Canadian tourist, but in Brownsville, there were lots of Mexicans. I showed my ID card and claimed asylum under the Cuban Adjustment Act.

With tears in my eyes, I clarified that I'd arrived there in the bed of a tractor, *and the sharks devoured my two companions, one of whom was just fifteen years old, and I have a relative in Miami, living right in Little Havana.*

They sent me to Florida, not on an airplane, but on a bus. I had my pockets bulging with all the money I'd taken from those three goons, so when I got to Miami, I went into a store and bought clothes so that my brother and the neighborhood's folks would find me presentable and not a total mess.

And that's how my life escaped me at thirty-one years of age, when I had so many things left to experience. All because of an air conditioner that, when I think about it, I didn't even need, since at my house we had no shortage of fans, but my mother insisted, *Amarilis, tell that cheap husband of yours that we need an air conditioner, there are people in the neighborhood who already have one and we can't fall behind everyone else*, and I went to look for it in Ciego like I was a goddamn mule, but in Ciego de Ávila there weren't any. *But in Cienfuegos*, my cousin who lives there told me on the phone, *they're all over the place, since it's the best city in Cuba after Havana and might even be better*, and my husband: *I don't have money for that*, while I: *If you don't give it to me, I'm leaving you, Eduardo, I'm leaving you, what are one hundred and fifty dollars to you, which is what I need to round out the six hundred*, and he looked at me from the bed with those disconcerted eyes, and then he went to the bank and gave me the rest for the air conditioner, and I went to Cienfuegos, to my cousin la Pepa's house, and you see how everything turned out, I couldn't see my daughter grow up or celebrate her fifteenth birthday with her as I'd dreamed; a good-looking *mulato* slit my throat and then abused my corpse. I couldn't attend my own burial. That night when I didn't arrive, la Pepa informed the police and called Chambas to tell my husband I was missing, and even though we were midharvest and tobacco requires a lot of care, my husband hired a gypsy cab and headed to Cienfuegos, but no matter how hard they looked, I didn't show up, eighteen months passed and they gave me up for disappeared, for an illegal immigrant via Mexico, there were also rumors that I'd fled with another man, and my parents and my sister Sabina and even la Pepa, who knew me as if I were her daughter, clung to that hope and already imagined me in concubinage with someone out by Minas de Zaza or harvesting apples in Delaware or somewhere else in the *Yuma*. Eduardo did take me for dead from the beginning, he knew I would never leave our daughter, because ever since she'd turned six years old, I'd been dreaming of celebrating her quinceañera, so he found it strange that I wouldn't reach out at all, not send a single e-mail, nothing, and when those bloodred boots he'd bought me for my twenty-fifth birthday showed up in a secondhand shop, he hugged them and told the police that now he was sure I was dead.

On May 10, 2009, my husband organized a symbolic burial, and in an empty box they placed my favorite dress, the boots, and a photo from my wedding.

Almost all of Chambas went to the cemetery.

MARIBEL

I saw them arrive. *Now Bertica's really fucked*, I thought. *She's become a lesbian.* At first, I thought that Araceli was American, she was so white and had that I-didn't-do-it face that gave me the creeps, but later when I went to investigate, she turned out to be just another starving Cuban, although that starving part is just a saying, because the girl had cash and loads of it, and with money, everything can be smoothed over, and Aurora, Bertica's mother, adjusted quite well to the girl's presence even though they only had one room and people were talking. Not me. People. *It's like a cathouse over there!* they would say. *In there, it's all the same if the mother sleeps with the daughter, if the mother is with the daughter's lesbian lover, if all three of them do it at once, anything goes over there at night.* They talked, but in reality, no one knew anything, and then one afternoon, I saw two well-dressed and well-put-together young women come out, and when I asked where they were going, Araceli told me they were going to Ian's workshop.

"Whose workshop? Are you going to fix a radio or a stove?"

"Poetry," they said. "We're going to learn poetry." And then I discovered that poetry can be learned.

I thought that those things couldn't be learned, that you're born a poet and that's that, but, no, I was floored by that, and later Prince joined them, since he was lonelier than the Devil ever since Gringo had left, and it wasn't enough for him to give sermons in front of that deranged cathedral that his father and the rest of the crazies never finished building. "The Black Cathedral," the people of Punta Gorda called it mockingly, the bastards. So fine, that favorite son also got into poetry and went out every Saturday with the two girls to the poets' workshop instead of devoting himself to his father's trade, as if there weren't already an artist in the family: that Johannes, who at the time was studying at the ISA in Havana and had an Italian boyfriend, a young guy, with long hair, tattoos, and pants that were ripped at both knees, who, still, was a nice guy and even went with the father as an equal to build the goddamn Black Cathedral. One time, I asked to borrow twenty dollars and he gave them to me without skipping a beat and told me not to repay him, not like that Johannes, who thought she was all that and never looked at anyone.

Both brothers studied at the high school right in the city,

it wasn't like before when students were forced to go to the countryside to become real men. You could see the Stuarts coming back in the afternoon and each going off to do his own thing: Cricket was good friends with Guts, who back then wasn't just jerking off anymore but spent his time exercising, he had a body that not even that Arnold Swazz-a-nayer could match. When I saw him, I would say, "*Mijito*, there's no food for all of this, the only muscle we women need is right down here," and I would look right at his fly and he would laugh, but one day, he knocked at my door, and I said, "What do you want, Guts? What's up?" And he went, "We're alone, Maribel, tell me now what that muscle is that women like," and I went, "You could be my son," and he went, "But I'm not, and I know every detail of your body," and I went, "Oh, yeah, Peeping Tom! Well then, what if I call the police?" And he went, "I could give a fuck about the police," and then he came close and I let him kiss me on the mouth, and then we fucked, but I didn't like it because he was too green for me, he was just a kid. The one I could have had a delicious screw with was Cricket, you could tell he had a really big one, that he had a terrifyingly large cock like my first husband, may he rest in peace, but Cricket didn't notice me, he was always kind of in love with his own sister. A really sad story, lovesick as a dog for Johannes, no one knew it then, but when what happened, happened, everything came out, and people started to put two and two together and said . . . they said lots of things, that there was a reason his father beat him, that this or that, but I know they're wrong, things aren't that simple. Cricket loved his sister, but silently, a platonic love like they say in romance novels, nobody knew it, the one who hinted at it to me was

Guts, who told me, *Cricket jerks off thinking of Johannes and sometimes steals her underwear and wraps it around the head of his cock.* Guts told me this after Cricket was already working at el Ruso's bar, charging foreigners, especially the lot of Russians who suddenly began to come through Cienfuegos, as much as he wanted to play out their sexual fantasies with Yusimí. The whole neighborhood knew what the kid was involved in when he started to wear expensive clothes and gold chains and slather himself with cream, shave off all his body hair, get manicures and his brows done; everyone in the neighborhood except for old Arturo Stuart and his wife, the latter because she was kind of a space cadet and the former because he was so focused on his cathedral that he barely noticed anything. When he found out, it was already too late, old Arturo wanted to give his son a beating like the ones that used to leave him stunned, but although Cricket continued to be sinewy, like a stick, it was no longer possible, Cricket was much taller than him, strong, and not afraid of him, and Cricket didn't believe in anything, less still in God and in that crappy building they called a temple that never finished being built. Arturo threw him out of the house. *Leave,* he said to him, *you're not my son anymore, cursed be the moment I conceived you.* What father says something like that to his son without considering the consequences? The kid took off, but he had money; also, el Ruso gave him a little room in the back of the bar for him to sleep in, a little room with an air conditioner, close to the girls' room, he only told him not to get involved with Magali since she belonged to Gordo Gris, and Gris wasn't understanding. "I'm not into men," people say Cricket replied. She's had an operation and now even has an ID card with a woman's name, el Ruso said. Once a man, always a man, Cricket kept saying and, with that, didn't leave it open for further discussion. No one knew about the human meat yet, so Salvador Pork Chop was still a well-regarded guy in the neighborhood, and since he won the lottery twice in a row, he was getting too big for his britches and didn't even look at black girls. He didn't even want light-skinned *mulatas*. He moved into the room Margot and her mother sold when they moved over by Martí Park and started bringing Punta Gotica's oldest and dirtiest white women there, whites and homos or transvestites as they're called, because Piggy was always a hell of a *bugarrón*, and while his boss, Gringo, lived in Cuba, Piggy held back, but now that Gringo wasn't there anymore, it was a free-for-all. He lost his looks when Guts beat the hell out of him. He got him in the middle of the alleyway, and there were blows any which way, and then he took out his prick and pissed on him in front of everyone. "El Ruso says to take him what you owe him," Guts said, and when he left, Piggy, without wiping the urine off himself, began to brag. *I'm really something*, he said, and came out with *My buddy Gringo and I had half of Punta Gorda eating dead person.*

Nobody seemed to believe him, but two days later a Lada from the DTI stopped at the entrance to the alleyway, and they carried off Pork Chop. He sang more than Pavarotti, and they gave him twenty years. They told Gringo over the phone. I think Nacho Fat-Lips was the one who told him. *Don't come around Cuba anymore, they know everything.*

I hated her smile full of teeth that looked perfect and turned out to be fake. I hated her son Jimmy, a middle-aged lazy ass who looked at me over his myopic glasses and confused Cuba with Haiti. I hated her little daughter Evelyn, too, even though I fucked her, I hated her from the start. When I seduced her that afternoon of barbecue and country music, here in Texas, at her husband's ranch, I fucked her every which way. I had to put my hand over her mouth so she wouldn't yell. "*Blanca puta, blanca puta,*" I whispered in her ear. She loved that, she had taken a Latin American literature class in Philadelphia and spoke a little Spanish, she was pretty the way Americans are, long legs, a sad doll's face, and no behind whatsoever, her lack of a posterior was worrying. But her tits were enormous and she knew how to show them off when she came up to me, on the arm of her husband, that meathead John Gordiner, an attorney, apparently.

"What did you study in Cuba, Richard?" Gordiner asked me that first time we saw each other at his ranch, Blue Bird, and I thought, *This guy's a* maricón, *only a* maricón *thinks of calling his place Blue Bird.*

"Construction technician," I replied, and smiled at the same time as if to say, *I'm the stupid black guy, you fucking gringo, who's going to enjoy your mother-in-law's money right here, that money saved up by the late Brian S. Pound, illustrious physician.*

"Are you two thinking of getting married?" the daughter asked me, in the most blatantly gossipy way, looking at her mother and me in a way that made me feel like I was still in Punta Gotica, talking to some old biddy in the neighborhood.

"We'll think about that later," my old lady replied, then laughed her laugh, like a giraffe in heat, that made me want to smack her.

I can't stand Americans and I knew it from the first, they're so full of themselves. Bullshit, second-class people are what they are.

I knew I was going to screw Evelyn, ever since she'd asked me, "Do you like literature? I have a lot of novels in Spanish and could lend you some."

"I love to read," I said, because American TV was horrific, and to get away from my old lady, Mrs. Elsa Pound, whose maiden name was Elsa Williams, I would do anything, I was so repulsed by her smell. That smell and the way she repeated "My God, my God!" when we screwed. Those would have been reasons enough to kill her; nevertheless, she didn't have a single freckle, her skin was white, smooth, and without many wrinkles, and she wasn't really very fat, at least not so much as to smell in that way that reminded me of fucking Piggy, who, according to what Nacho told me on the phone, broke and ratted me out, screwing himself in the process. They didn't execute him, but he did get twenty years. That Piggy will die a miserable man, never getting far, after all.

BERTA

Given subsequent events, it seems strange, but it's not strange since we're talking about the Stuarts. I started reading a lot. Because my house was too small, Araceli and I would go to Martí Park and take several books, almost always poetry, but also novels. One day I'm alone at the park, reading Marguerite Yourcenar for the first time in my life (Araceli was hiding, her ex-husband was in Cienfuegos, looking for her, and until he left town, she had rented an apartment close to the police headquarters in the Tulipán neighborhood), when I heard someone approaching me. I lifted my head and there was Prince.

"Introduce me to your teacher."

"Okay," I said, and that Saturday I went to get him early and took him to the Dionisio San Román bookstore and introduced him to the other aspiring poets and to Ian.

Ten months later, he published his first poem in a Havana literary magazine, before me and everyone else. Of course, he had always been a reader, and a writer, too. While I was still listening to ballads in English and playing with dolls, he was already trying his hand at verse.

All his poems were about the same thing, death.

The Deacon, that's what we called him in the workshop, even Ian sometimes called him that. Something clerical about him didn't go with his age. Even if things hadn't gone in that direction, so sordid, Prince would have still gone mad.

Of all the Stuarts, the only one who could have passed for normal was Johannes, who also wrote poetry. A few months ago, when I was at the Rome Book Fair, at a gallery near the Cuba stand, I saw one of her paintings, perhaps the best-known one, *Cathedral*, it's called, and it's an interpretation of her parents' temple. I knew that after what happened, happened, she had changed her name. Judith, she's called now, another biblical name, it's crazy, right? At three in the afternoon, my book was being presented and I would have liked to invite her, but she didn't recognize me, she didn't even seem to see me, although we were the only two young black women in that entire modern art gallery.

She was dressed like a Hollywood actress and was with her husband at the time, Vicenzo Albertino, the Naples soccer player, a blond guy who didn't seem like much to me, despite having shoulder-length hair and light-colored eyes. Vicenzo was her third or fourth husband, I don't know, I'm not keeping track. Now she's a renowned painter, but the true genius in that family was Prince, only he was mad.

BÁRBARO

I don't know why I was getting so curvy, but Piggy comes to me one day and says, "We have to talk about something very important, come to my room so we're both comfortable."

Until then, I had only talked to him maybe twice, at most, and I blurted out, "What's wrong with you?"

But he didn't get too worked up, and said, "Come by and knock five times tonight, so I'll know it's you, and open the door quick."

I waited until ten at night, and what happened, happened. When I got there, Salvador had a bottle of Havana Club, two little cans of soda, and a glass of ice on top of the table. He put on music on a small CD player and asked me to unwind. I agreed, he served me a drink with lots of soda in it, like I like it, and I drank it, then he asked me to dance.

"I'm going to the bathroom," I said when the song was over, because I felt a little dizzy.

"Don't go down the toilet," he said jokingly, and when I came back to the living room, he had his cock in his hand.

"Take a look and see if you like it," he said, and I liked it, so I knelt down.

But before sucking it, I said, "Don't come in my mouth."

BERTA

That he was in love with his sister, I don't believe that. Cubans are like that, always looking to put a melodramatic shine on everything; after all, we grew up steps from a temple that they never finished building, and besides, if it had been built, what good would it do? Another monument to nothingness, although, of course, I'm not the best person to talk about Cricket. After he left home, I barely saw him, I wasn't crazy enough to go over to el Ruso's bar, perhaps the most infamous place in Cienfuegos.

GRINGO

It's hard for me to pinpoint the exact moment I started to get sick of my old lady, but one day I asked myself how long I could put up with her, and the answer was that I couldn't anymore, I had to free myself of her. We had settled in Houston, and I had started working with my stepdaughter's husband, I was something like the foreman or one of the shift managers at that scrap-processing plant of which Elsa was one of the main investors. I had to wake up early every day, get dressed, and go to work, but beforehand, of course, I had to get the old lady off. My only real distraction was running, I'd gotten big on exercising, and every afternoon, after work, I would put on my special sneakers and go out to run around the outskirts of the city. I read a lot, my stepdaughter kept supplying me with books. With Evelyn, I did like screwing. We would use a variety of excuses to go out to Blue Bird and we would do our thing there. Sometimes I had fun calling Cienfuegos, pretending to be someone else. Once, I had Maribel waiting for a package that turned out to be an extra-large vibrator. "Have yourself some fun," I put on the paper I sent with the box. Maribel sold it to el Ruso, since the vibrator was one of the good ones, and our *tovarish* needed it to get more money out of his girls, Berta later told me, she still didn't know about my dealings with human flesh since Piggy hadn't broken yet and I was still looked up to in the neighborhood. Not even in Houston was there a bar like el Ruso's, so satisfying, although it's true I should admit that the girls here, at first glance, were better, almost all of them blond with big tits, but in the end those tits were filled with silicone and many of them weren't even women. Here, you're forced to be careful about almost everything.

What I liked best from my whole time in Houston was meeting this Indian chick who used to run along the same road I did, and who I saved from some useless piece of shit. I just had to kick the guy's chest so he would leave, and she repaid me with sex. She hadn't yet turned twenty-five, she was kind of skinny and had no ass, but she had these small tits with purple nipples that fit perfectly in my mouth, knew how to speak French, and read me Bukowski poems. I liked that. I also liked that she considered me a refined, classy guy and thought I had gone to college. Just because I'd read Vargas Llosa and Javier Marías, she thought I was an intellectual. Nadine, that was her name, and she believed that the United States needed to disband, and when she got to talking about that, she would

121

go on and on as if it were the worst place in the world. She was proud of being Apache, although you could tell she wasn't pure-blood, her mom was from Quebec. Sometimes when we had sex, I would yell in Spanish at her, *"¡Gran jefa india yegua salvaje!"* She understood the joke and would laugh. If I had had money, I would have stayed with Nadine, but to see my plans through, I needed to take my old lady, Elsa Pound, away from Houston, out of Texas even. I started talking to her about Kentucky and its blue fields, and saying I wanted to breed horses, and through looking on the Internet, I even found a good, cheap ranch for sale, near Louisville.

Now, as I think of that, I wonder how someone that old—Elsa had just turned sixty-six—could be such a fool, and I have no answer. To think that such a young man—I was only twenty-eight years old—had fallen in love upon seeing her in a grocery store is naïve enough, but to take out a life insurance policy in that young man's name and then leave the place where all of your properties are, where your husband of many years is buried, and move far away from your only family, requires a healthy dose of idiocy or an out-of-control taste for black dick. It almost inspired pity. *But you've got to live*, I said to myself, and when we moved, I let two years go by when I practically became a cowboy from riding horses so much. My favorite one was a mare called Boise, whose nimble gait and jet-colored pelt reminded me of Johannes. For a while, I also became a fan of races and even saw the Derby. The horse breeders didn't have any respect for me; they thought, rightly so, that the only mare I had tamed was Mrs. Elsa Pound.

One summer afternoon, I said to her, "Darling, I need to

go to Miami to see my brother. I'm going in six days, but I'll be back right away."

She didn't feel well, diabetes was doing quick work on her, so she agreed.

"I'll stay with Melody," she said. "Do not worry." Melody was the maid, a Vietnamese girl who was almost invisible, she was so small and thin.

"Okay," I said, and on the Thursday of the trip, I left in one of the cars in the direction of the airport.

I got about five hundred or so yards from the house. I made a U-turn. I jumped the fence. The dogs, since they knew me, didn't bark. I climbed to the second-floor bathroom window, which I had left open to get in, and made the most of the fact that my old lady, at that hour of the day, tended to relax in her Jacuzzi listening to music, and I pushed the small CD player into the tub and she was electrocuted. Then I went out the window again. I took the car. I got to Louisville. I left the car in a lot near the airport and I boarded the plane headed to Miami.

The next day, Melody, blabbering in an English that was difficult to understand, informed me by cell phone that I was a widower and had to return urgently to Sweet Grass, that was what our ranch was called.

The burial was in Houston, and from the beginning, when they saw the size of the insurance policy, they suspected me, although they limited themselves to giving me dirty looks and making it clear I wasn't part of the family. They didn't understand how my wife could have thought to leave me $150,000 hard cash; in addition, she left me the ranch. To Evelyn and her brother, she left everything else: the shares in the scrap-processing plant, the enormous suburban house, and an apartment right in Manhattan; still, that wasn't enough for them.

After the funeral, I rented a room in one of the city's best hotels and called Nadine.

I spent my time screwing to forget my pain. I would have taken her with me, but in my absence, Nadine's inclination toward terrorism had increased and she talked about killing thousands of "federal fucking pigs" and of snuffing out some immigrants through a bomb she'd place at Houston Stadium.

"I already have the C-4 for it, but I just have to get the cell ready. Help us, Richard, I can tell you know about weapons, what do you say?"

"Annihilating immigrants like me?"

"Not like you."

"You're a crazy bitch," I said, thinking that I, who had only wiped out four people, was nothing but a snot-nosed boy explorer compared to her and her minions.

A week later, I'd cashed out my policy and left for Kentucky to sell the ranch to the only one of the other landowners I liked: an old guy, the son of an Austrian Jew who'd been gassed under Hitler. The hardest thing was saying goodbye to my mare Boise.

CLARO ARGÜELLES QUESADA, *former Poder Popular delegate in Punta Gotica*

From the beginning, they should have been clear with them, told them, *No, you're not going to spend the province's limited resources on that mad temple, no, and that's final.* But they were cowards, they were afraid they would be accused of being racist and antireligious—even more so since in the beginning, when the American pastor put down the first ten thousand dollars, Stuart and Basulto made sure that the presence of the Holy Sacrament congregation, or the Sacramentalists, as people called them, was felt at every event reaffirming the Revolution. It was a wise move. You couldn't organize anything for the anniversary of the Committees for the Defense of the Revolution without them showing up. They were the first ones to donate blood. They went to do volunteer work and to the May 1 and July 26 parades. The only thing I couldn't get from them was their participation in an event repudiating one of those so-called independent journalists. They flat out refused to attend. I latched onto that and went to see the president of Poder Popular and said to him:

"If you'll excuse me, *compañero presidente*, they've been building that temple for ten years and there's no end in sight; if it keeps growing, it's going to exceed this very building in height and that wouldn't be good . . . On the other hand, they're wasting necessary resources for social projects; many of the homes in the neighborhood are falling to pieces."

"They pay in dollars and on time, so don't worry," the president said to me.

"Yes, but it's not just the money. It's also the ideological character of this construction; imagine, to allow that church is to give the enemy more power, they've even been featured on a program in Miami, one called *Sábado Gigante*."

"Sábado Gigante?" the president asked me. "Do you watch those things?"

"No, not me, I saw it by accident."

"And what did they say on this *Sábado*?"

"That in Cienfuegos, we're crazy, that communism must have gone to our heads if we're allowing the blacks to make a cathedral."

"You see, delegate," the president said. "That's the point, in Cienfuegos, we're erecting the first cathedral that is truly for and by the meek, even the enemy has to recognize it."

"Yes, but the thing is that it was never a Black Cathedral, *compañero presidente*, and you'll excuse me, that cathedral belongs to that crazy Holy Sacrament congregation, and it may have grown a lot in recent times, but I can assure you that it doesn't have twenty thousand members, and the majority only come for the snacks and the American donations."

"So what? What matters is what people think, remember that this is a *Battle of Ideas*."

I was about to resign right there as a Poder Popular delegate in Punta Gotica; it rubbed me the wrong way that intelligent people, aware of how things work in this world, would fall for such a mirage. I knew that to permit the Sacramentalist cathedral was to condemn that neighborhood and Cienfuegos itself to failure, in spite of the tourists who didn't ask anymore where the Reina Cemetery was, or Martí Park or Jagua Hotel, but came here to Punta Gotica and swooned over the crumbling houses, the people sitting on the sidewalk right in the middle of the workday, the blaring music, and the filth. All to photograph a building that never got finished and that reminded me a little of Juraguá's nuclear power plant, another failure. *How long can this go on?* I thought, watching as the neighborhood filled up with little stands and used-book vendors, all to have something to sell to the foreigners.

In addition, that Arturo Stuart now thought he was a tough guy, he seemed like more of a Poder Popular delegate than I did. He thought he was some kind of mayor. If someone needed medication, they went to see him; if an alcoholic's family wanted to take his house away, they went to see him. I was practically little more than a decorative object, and his kids, well, the three of them were unbelievable; one, Johannes, with that little Italian boyfriend who would come up beeping in his Willys jeep, waking up the neighbors and propagating an ideology he didn't believe in. I went to see the exposition she organized in the ruins of the Goytisolo Palace, and, well, the truth is that the girl has talent as a painter, but what is all that? Those loose women wrapped in the nation's flag? I don't know how they allowed it, really. No wonder she left for Italy and never came back, she was always a *gusana*, a worm. As far as the other kid is concerned, the one called Prince, he still hadn't shown his claws yet, but we already knew he would be a case, we already knew. You would see him go by with those little poetry books under his arm and that good-boy face, and you wouldn't be able to comprehend how he could be initiated into Palo, could be superstitious, so removed from the necessary dialectic vision of the world, just like the rest of the Stuart family. Initiated into Palo and still preaching at the Church of the Holy Sacrament, I don't know how his father didn't catch on, well, it's incredible. Of course, the worst was the other one, that one was already pegged as one of the neighborhood's juvenile delinquents, a personal friend of Antón Abramovich, alias el Ruso, the worst of his kind in Punta Gotica and the whole city, a foreigner that the Revolution should have deactivated a long time ago, but who, without a doubt, had connections in the highest spheres, since his bar / gambling den / restaurant was the most corrupt place in the city, and things went on as usual . . .

FERREIRO

I went to Cienfuegos three times, looking for Araceli. The first time was because her own father asked me to. The other two, on my own account, at my own risk. I never found her, to tell the truth. She knew how to hide. But years later, I was having some drinks with my buddies when Manolo says to me, *Hey, Alcibíades, that one really looks like Araceli.* I look at the TV and notice a blonde who's giving the meteorological report, and though she was wearing more makeup and looked classier, it could only be her. *Fuck*, I thought, but I didn't say anything, I acted indifferent. I know she left me out of spite because someone told her I was with Elisa.

In those early days, if I had found her, I would have disgraced myself. I was in such a state that if you'd stuck a needle in me, I wouldn't have bled. I took Araceli from her home when she was fifteen, and I was her first husband. We were so hopeful when we married, our wedding was a high-end event, I invited some mariachis from Santa Clara, who even sang the fucking "Mañanitas del rey David," and then we went to Varadero and spent our honeymoon at the Hotel Internacional at a time when it was rare to see a Cuban around there, I spent nearly eighty thousand pesos on those nuptials, but it didn't bother me: Araceli was the most beautiful thing in town and she was mine. Our disagreements started when she told me

128

she wanted to keep going to school, as if being married to a man like me, with money and properties, wasn't enough for her, but I gave in. *If you want to study, then go ahead, get to it,* I said to her, *take a waitressing course or something like that, it could always be useful,* but, no, she wanted to finish high school and go on to college and act important, and I didn't like that, although I agreed to it; in the end, she spent all day reading, mostly poetry, and she talked to me as if she thought she was better than me, and the strangest thing in the world was, I also thought that in a way she had something different about her than all the other women I'd been with before, she was, like, classier and more sensitive, and I was naïve enough to think that because of that, I could trust her. So to find out that in addition to having left me, she was a lesbian in Cienfuegos, it was hard for me, really. I would have preferred to see her dead, and that's what I told her parents.

"Tell her that if she comes around here, I don't want to see her, because if I see her, I'll ignore her; what she did to me, you don't do that to a man."

Her brother jumped out like a fighting cock. *If you touch her, Ferreiro, I'll kill you,* he said to me, but I looked him in the eye, and he had to bow his head in shame: a man who defends a lesbian and a whore isn't worth anything, even if the witch is his sister, and especially since I'd given her everything. She didn't want for anything with me, she was the apple of my eye, but she failed me in the end and she disrespected me and I thought I would never forgive her, that I was going to spend the rest of my life looking for her, but it wasn't like that, I went to Cienfuegos three times to look for her, but then I got tired,

I didn't go anymore, although people looked down on me like I wasn't a real man, as if I wasn't capable of satisfying a woman and that was why she left me. Isn't that something?

I kept an eye out for her, she was very close to her mother and I was sure that one day I'd see her crossing these streets, but it didn't happen that way. She never returned to Cabaiguán, or at least not that I saw.

GRINGO

Margaret was a much tougher conquest than picking up Elsa. She was fifty-seven years old, and when I met her, she was all dressed in black latex, so beautiful from far off that she looked like she'd escaped from a version of *Charlie's Angels*, but by then, Margaret wasn't even fit for vultures anymore. She was keen on motorcycles. She had a shop where she sold the best Italian bikes, but what she really adored were Harleys, and she was from Memphis, Tennessee, where Elvis Presley lived, and where, of course, they killed Martin Luther King.

I saw her get off her Harley, which seemed brand-new, and go into her shop.

I followed her, thinking she was just another customer, but when I saw the employees bending over backward to show her how efficient they were, I understood that she was the owner or the main shareholder. I went up to one of the motorcycles on display, a Ducati that looked like a spaceship, and pretended to be interested, but in reality, I was watching her. An employee came up to me, a young black guy with the face of a trained dog.

"The best," he said to me in English, with indifference. "It has an elevated dual exhaust, a single-sided swing arm, mono-bloc brakes, and 560 cc for the most powerful twin-cylinder engine ever sold."

"I also used to sell motorcycles in Cuba," I said to gain his trust.

"Oh, really. Ducatis?"

"No, no way, MZT, Jawas, Carpatis, and Benjovinas."

"Really, I don't know those brands . . ."

"Well, they were very good . . . Who's that woman, man?" I pointed at Margaret, who was talking to another employee, a white, blond-haired one who I didn't like the looks of from the start.

"That one?" the *yuma* asked me as if he were deaf.

"Yes, of course."

"That's Margaret O'Sullivan, the owner of the store. I'm surprised you don't know her."

"Why would I know her?"

"Everyone here in Louisville knows her . . . she was the 500 cc world champion . . ."

"Well then . . ." To gain time, I asked him to tell me a little more about the motorcycle.

She came up to us. The thing is, I was dressed as if I'd just gotten one of those stars they put on Hollywood Boulevard, I had money and good taste and that opens all doors in Cuba and this country as well, to be honest.

"Hello," she said, stretching out her long, dry hand.

"Hi." I shook it and looked straight into those gray old-lady eyes that had a twinkle of youth.

"Give us a minute, Timothy," she said, without looking at the employee.

Cubans are everywhere; all of them are or say they are artists. Even though you see them collecting garbage on Las Ramblas or as bathroom attendants at a nightclub, they say they are artists and poets. If Berta were here, she would love it, because she always had an artistic soul, like a writer and all that. I'll tell you that I didn't really like seeing her become a lesbian. That little white girl, Araceli, didn't have much of a body, but she had a face prettier than anything I've seen over here in Europe. She and Berta were a good couple. I didn't believe it when the rumors started. I think it was Piggy, to get in good with me, who told me, *Berta's a lesbian*, and I said to him, *Sure, she's banging your mother*, but later I saw how the two of them looked at each other. I think Berta's mother never accepted it.

You've got to be tougher here than in Cienfuegos, any druggie has a gun and will shoot you over any little thing, it's not like over there, although the truth is that el Ruso was having problems from the start, he was too opportunistic for my liking, despotic, nothing ever seemed right to him and he usually treated people like dogs. I still remember how he drawled his words and would start talking shit about how in Moscow, how in Saint Petersburg, as if we didn't know he was actually Ukrainian. Here in Barcelona there are also a lot of Ukrainians, they're worse than the Arabs, no one's more deceptive and fast-talking. I was with a chick from Kiev, superhot and all that, Irina with the blue eyes, but within a month she'd filled my house with people, and her father liked to play the accordion. I hate the accordion. One day, I hid it, and that's as far as things got, Irina and I had a tremendous fight, it was awful. I had a brawl with her older brother, Oleg was his name, he had been a sailor with the Black Sea fleet, but he couldn't take me on, I won. I really knocked him in that Misha-the-Bear nose of his and then got my gun from the trunk and pointed it at all three of them. "You leave here right now," I told them, and they started speaking in Ukrainian and crying, but then they got out.

"Go sleep on Las Ramblas," I repeated, by way of goodbye.

But getting back to Mr. Antón Abramovich, Ukrainian Cuban, whom we all called el Ruso, I never liked him. He had this scornful little way about him, just unbearable, and when Cricket came to work with us, things got worse. Cricket liked Yusimí with the light-colored eyes, and el Ruso, who was sly and greedy down to his bones, noticed, and I was in the middle, since Cricket, being from Camagüey and all, was my lifelong friend, and in my innocence, I thought there was something like honor in the world. That if I defend you, you defend me. That if I'm your brother, you're my brother. I was wrong. Because Cricket had no friends. It seems that old man Stuart's beatings had taken his manhood away, I don't know, or it seems that he really was in love with Johannes, and something about him was weird, he wasn't a man of honor. He acted like el Ruso's damn slave. He disappointed me, and when everything went rotten, he picked el Ruso, and el Ruso had no scruples and let them put him in prison.

El Ruso watched as the cathedral went up and he wanted the Sacramentalists to give us something. "To protect them," he said, "so that no one steals their materials and slows down their work."

He called Gordo Gris and me, and he told us to talk to

Basulto and explain that he, Antón Abramovich, had to be shown respect; he needed some kind of compensation for not having decided to erect an Orthodox church in the middle of Punta Gotica. After all, the Arabs could come and talk to the Poder Popular president and erect a mosque at any point, and that shouldn't be allowed, how could it be, but you know, to him, Antón Abramovich, they were all the same: a guy from Camagüey or a Jew or a guy from the eastern part of the island, or an Arab, so they should understand, there were rules to be followed in Cienfuegos. "Come on," Gordo Gris said to me, and we got in the jeep and went to see that Basulto, a little white nothing of a man who was nonetheless good at dodging blows.

"I don't have anything to do with that," he said. "The treasurer is brother Stuart, go see him."

Gordo always wore gray and was always sad. He had been a policeman in Matanzas, and he killed a guy during carnival because he called him "whale." They gave him ten years. In prison, he got his nickname, Gordo Gris. He didn't get out until fourteen years later because he nearly killed another guy. He came to Cienfuegos, and el Ruso hired him right away. He was light-skinned and could pass for white. He liked to beat up blacks, and if they were blacks who were good with the ladies, even more so: he hadn't fucked a real female since the days of President Machado. He had a small prick. He didn't show it to any of the whores, and he threatened Magali, *If you tell anyone, I'll kill you.* He took out his rage on blacks. He was dying to give Cricket a beating, but Cricket was sacred. El Ruso wouldn't let anyone touch him, and Cricket, when he'd tossed back a few, would laugh at Gordo Gris, he called him fatty and an old bitch of an ex-con. That's why, when we were told that we had to go see Cricket's dad, Gordo Gris was happy.

"We're going to strip that old black man down to nothing."

"It's not going to be easy," I said. "We have to be diplomatic."

"That's your job," he said.

GRINGO

Give us a minute, Timothy.

That's how these American women are, when they don't need you, you become a nothing, like a Ducati with legs. They think they're competitive, but at heart they're just fools. They're so scared of lies that the majority of them don't know how to spot a liar, anyone can pull one over on them. Here you can say you're selling land on the moon, and there will always be a few morons to buy it from you.

My money was running out, it's incredible how much you have to spend to maintain the standard of living I was used to after marrying Elsa, and this Margaret sweated money. I asked her how much the Ducati was.

"Fifty-five thousand with an initial deposit of twenty thousand . . . We include the accessories; in other words, a whole mechanic's kit and a black racing-team jacket."

"What about in cash?"

"In cash, it's fifty thousand. I came over to see to you myself because I can tell you have good taste, and this motorcycle is very special to me, it's the best Italy has designed, and believe me, you won't regret it."

"Okay, I'm going to think about it . . . Are you the manager?" I asked as if I didn't care, and she clarified that she was the main shareholder and founder of the shop.

"Congratulations, your store has a lot of style."

She looked me in the eye, then she looked at my clothes, you could tell she was thinking something like *Who the hell does this asshole think he is?* I almost liked it, actually, on her own she was nothing special, thin as a rail, but she had an ass, not much, but for an American it was something.

I could have told her I was African and that I was part of my country's nobility, but I thought that athletes love other athletes, so I casually mentioned that I played baseball, and she wrinkled her cold little nose and made a sigh of disdain. *She hates blacks*, I thought, but then she asked if what I had on my wrist was an *ildé*.

"Of course, I'm a Babalawo."

Margaret rolled up the sleeve of her black jacket and showed me her forearm, around which she also wore a blue-beaded *ildé*.

"Yemayá," I said, and she opened up to me like a flower. She took me to the shop's bar, and there, surrounded by the images of motorcycles that had won a bunch of championships and rallies, she started to tell me about the time she had spent in Bahía, where she had practiced Candomblé, some sort of Brazilian witchcraft, since she was married to Enzo Campeiro, a Formula One racer she'd met in Morocco at a championship organized by the king, and who was later one of the thousands killed on September 11, 2001.

"Ever since then, you hate Arabs," I interrupted her, but she said no, that what she was afraid of, terrified of, were extremists, no matter where they came from, and that Bush and all of his super-Christian and Republican buddies got her out of sorts.

"They're turning this country to shit," she said.

She was talking and I was taking sips of vermouth and nodding my head yes, trying to avoid sticking my foot in my mouth again, since this kind of woman can be hell to deal with if you start talking nonsense. You can't deny this about American women, they're classy, even if ultimately they're all the same. They spend their days doing things for other people, helping black Haitians, or collecting money for unhappy Thais, et cetera, et cetera, that's how they are; in the end, Margaret was something special, it was a shame I'd met her when she was already so old, since in the pictures decorating the walls, she looked like a movie star, riding on her Harley with a smile ear to ear and a flower wreath around her neck: CHAMPION OF THE CASABLANCA–RABAT RALLY.

"The accident happened after that." She told me about her fall, not from a motorcycle, but from a car going over ninety miles an hour on the French Riviera, days after finding out that Enzo had died. "They operated on me in Seattle." She looked at me with wide eyes.

While looking into her gray irises, I couldn't help but inquire with a sigh, "And then?"

"I had to get a prosthesis."

She rolled up her tight pants and showed me her leg, not a plastic one like a doll's, like the kind you see in Cuba, where almost all the lame go around on just one leg, and if they're lucky, they get a stiff prosthesis, but rather a sophisticated robotic extremity made of carbon fiber.

I was happy that Margaret was missing a leg.

I had exactly $175,493 left, and that's nothing here, it's practically condemning you to become a pizza delivery boy; besides, I had to pay for a new identity, I couldn't go on being the widower of the deceased Elsa Pound, since these *yumas* don't forget, and credible papers that you can show without trembling in your boots are expensive.

ILEANA

I had to deal with that Johannes for over ten years, and when I say deal with, it's because we started at the Basic School for Visual Arts in Cienfuegos, the Benny Moré School, and later we continued at the ENA, and in the end we were at the ISA, and all that time, we thought we were something like friends. Although I now ask myself what our friendship consisted of, since Johannes only had time for one thing: her work. From the beginning, she was an anointed one. When we were still at the Basic School, she spent more time on her creations than any of the rest of us. At the ISA, that quality became more pronounced; we two were the only ones from Cienfuegos in our year, but nonetheless, we interacted very little. I've always been a conceptual artist, with little interest in the artisanal, and I was interested in what was contemporary. But I still hadn't defined my way of approaching art. Johannes already knew what she wanted. She had a method she called *anti-Kacho*: it consisted of submitting herself to laborious work that began with her writing in a notebook, going on to a photography phase, then she sketched, and after that, on to the canvas, where she applied what she called *layers of reality*. Those layers of reality were made of oils superimposed with such refinement that, when Johannes finished a painting, what came to mind were the great masters of the late Renaissance. When Johannes decided to show you some of her paintings, you'd think of the Venetian school. Due to that almost mannerist quality of her creations, she was criticized by the faculty at the institute. The teachers didn't understand the need, in these times of high-definition photography, to paint in such detail. They criticized her so much, but she never gave up her creative method. In the end, she ended up being accepted. Imagine, she participated in the Havana Biennial when she was only in her second year, and at *Arte Cubano* magazine, one of their most important critics took the trouble to publish a review of her work, along with photos. I still have a copy of that magazine, since Johannes gave it to me. It was one of the few nice things she did for me.

She never talked about her family, and less still about the cathedral. I have always lived in Punta Gorda, which is the better part of the city, by far. I seldom went to Punta Gotica; for me, like so many other people in Cienfuegos from good families, the city ended to the left of Martí Park. *You're not missing much over there*, my late father, may he be in glory, would say, and he boasted that he'd never been to Punta Gotica. But when the church of the brothers of the Holy Sacrament, the Black Cathedral, as the people called it, started to take shape, I would ride my bicycle out to see what had always seemed like the best work in the city of Cienfuegos to me: an exceptional piece of visual art. At that time, I was with the guy who would later be Johannes's first husband. His girlfriend without our ever having seen each other. I met Guido in one of those many chat rooms on the Internet, and after several virtual meetings

139

where we found out we had many things in common, from our love of rock and heroic fantasy novels to German expressionist films, I sent him a photo and he wanted to come add a physical dimension to our electronic empathy. Okay, I said, and a week later, Guido set foot in Cienfuegos. He was tall, about thirty years old, narrow in the hips, with good pecs, a *mango*, as you would say these days. I introduced him to my family and they loved him. They especially liked that he wasn't Neapolitan, they have such a bad reputation in Cienfuegos, but rather, he was from Lombardy. Guido was from Milan itself, the most industrialized city in Italy. When I took him to see the Black Cathedral, he was fascinated. He took a thousand pictures and told me that we Cubans were crazy. Guido worked as the manager at a bank, and he was like that, so expressive, that he seemed Cuban. I introduced him to Arturo Stuart, he was there with the other workers, working shirtless, and Guido was surprised by how his muscly torso contrasted with his gray hair and wrinkled face. He looks like an old mercenary, Guido whispered to me, when the old man, after wishing us blessings, shook our hands and went back to his work laying bricks. He's the father of a friend of mine from school, I made the mistake of saying. He wanted to meet her, and when we were back in Havana and I took him to the ISA dorms and introduced them, everything ended between us. He liked Johannes. She had that quality that attracted a lot of foreigners, especially if they were European. To many Cubans, Johannes was just one more black girl, pretty enough, but too dark for our tastes. With outsiders, everything was in her favor; she was so proud, she seemed like an Egyptian princess. Many people thought she was a dance student, not a visual artist. To sum things up, she took my boyfriend. She did it her way, as if she didn't realize it, making herself to be innocent. He invited her out and she went. Later, if I asked her, she would say, looking at me with those brown eyes of hers, *We were talking about art, he wants to buy a painting from me.* Hypocrite. One day I was resolved and asked her to fight. I said, *Look, black whore, let's make the most of it being Sunday and no one being at the school, let's close the dorm and hit each other until we decide who Guido belongs to, because you're not going to ruin my damn life.* I said all of that, and she, cold as she was, told me that she had taken karate in her early teen years, over there in Camagüey, and a fight wasn't in my best interest: *I'll knock you into outer space, and as for Guido, you can have him with a side of fries, it's not my fault he's chasing after me.* When I heard all this, I pounced on her, but they pulled us apart. Later, we spent a long time without speaking to each other. Guido left for Europe. Six months went by, and when I wrote to him, he was cold toward me. In the end, I wrote him an e-mail clarifying that I wasn't anybody's leftovers and telling him to go to hell. He replied that was fine.

When he returned from Italy, he was already Johannes's boyfriend. He would go pick her up at the dorm and they would kiss practically in my face, and, well, it was so enormously disrespectful that one day I put a Nirvana song on the MP4 and took some pills so I could just float away. Some roommates saved me. I spent a fair bit of time seeing a psychologist at the Hermanos Ameijeiras Hospital and ended up understanding the serious mistake I was about to make, ending my life because of those two thoughtless people, especially her, who was supposed to be my friend. I've already forgiven her; after all, she has suffered enough, despite being a millionaire. Money and fame don't take anyone's pain away, that much is clear to me.

GRINGO

I had gotten hooked on nightlife. I liked a little Chilean whore, Mía, who had been an acrobat in the Cirque du Soleil, and now she had classy and selective customers. I wasn't a customer to her, I was something like a lover, but she had even more expensive taste than I did, and although she insisted on paying, many times I was the one who dropped the dough, so she wouldn't think I was a *pazguato*, and to uphold my country's honor here with pride, so far away from lovely little Cuba, in this Louisville, the northernmost city in the South, where everyone just thinks about horses and fancies that they're from the Wild West. I had become sophisticated, I, who had spent my childhood in flip-flops. I covered my whole body in the moisturizer recommended by a famous actor, and I got a manicure once a month, and I went to races and bet, very little, but I bet all the same, all to rub shoulders with loaded women, so that I knew the hippest places in Louisville and was known in them, since I've always been a generous tipper, so when the waiters saw me come in with Margaret on my arm, they bent over backward to serve us, some covertly winked at me, the idiots, since Margaret, although she looked good for her age, was a hag in comparison to me, who spent my days running and at the gym, boxing with a trainer who protected my face.

I really did like that little Chilean chick; actually, she had turned thirty already and was depressive, sometimes she would cry since she was very Catholic and she was ashamed of having sunk so low, that was why she wasn't going back to her country, so I told her to lie like everyone else does, to say she was a crocodile hunter in the swamps of Zapata.

"And where's that?"

"In Cuba, but while they work out where it is, they'll start getting used to the idea that you were a whore."

BERTA

Sometimes we got out of the workshop early, and Prince would invite us to have ice cream. The line was very long, so Araceli, he, and I would sit on the Prado to wait and we'd talk. I didn't love him anymore and could look at his face without feeling those old butterflies. Now I admired him a lot. He seemed destined for great things, especially if he managed to focus, make poetry the center of his life, and forget about preaching at that crazy church of his father's. Those were beautiful days. Araceli had told me she loved me. She said it one afternoon when we were alone at my house, reading Ángel Escobar, and I didn't know what to say. I'd never had relations with any woman, but her mouth smelled like almonds, and smells are important to me. I had spent a lifetime suffering the bad breath of my neighborhood's various drunks. I had promised myself never to kiss anyone who smelled like alcohol, cigarettes, indigestion, or cavities.

Araceli was perfect. Despite having been married and even having cheated on her husband, she had something virginal, innocent about her that was even reflected in her poems, the majority of them written in prose. Poems that the teacher would critique a lot since they weren't urbane, nor did they

143

seem like they were created by someone so young. I really do like Araceli's poetry, including the majority of her work as a teenager. When we've seen each other again, now she works in television, I've asked her about her early writings and she hasn't known what to say. It has been easier for her to propose—*Sleep with me, please, I need it so, so much*—than to talk about her poetry. That's normal in Cuba, your light goes out and then you're afraid to turn it on again. *One day, we're going to write a novel together*, she proposed, the last time we saw each other, there in the TV studio where her program is broadcast from. She was made-up to go on air, that's why her face reminded me of a geisha's.

"A novel that covers everything, from the cathedral to the Stuart brothers, including our love, because we really loved each other, right? I never imagined I would love a woman and less still one named Berta; meeting each other changed our lives, right?"

"Yes. What about Aramís? Will Aramís be in your novel?"

She didn't reply since at that moment the producer came over to tell her only three minutes were left. She blew me a kiss and said, *Later we'll definitely see each other, wait for me, we'll go in the car to see the Carlos Varela concert.*

"Okay," I assured her. Later didn't happen, I left.

But that afternoon on the bench in the Prado in Cienfuegos with our dreams almost intact, waiting our turn at the Coppelia ice cream shop in Cienfuegos, we would listen to young Prince and it seemed like everything was going to be different. Now I understand that was one of the few peaceful periods gifted to us by life: Araceli's husband was no longer hauling himself out to Cienfuegos with the sole purpose of killing her for being a whore and a lesbian. Prince was far from being the monster he would later become; my mother was alive; and I was happy. Not in a thunderous, showy way; I was quietly happy little by little, in small pieces, almost without being aware of it. I read a lot. The three of us read a lot, and truly, I didn't worry about how I would soon start to like women. I loved feeling Araceli's breath on my face, bathing in that breath, everything else slid off of me.

GRINGO

She talked a lot for an American. By the second date, I already knew her parents' names and that she had a brother who also raced sports cars, who lived in Monte Carlo. She talked, but she watched you with inquisitive eyes, penetrating you, assessing each of your words, and barely gave you the chance to touch her. Three weeks went by before she would let me graze her lips with mine. The thing was, she had a complex about our notable age difference and her being lame.

"I found my twin soul in you," she confirmed at last after our first tongue kiss, and I looked at her with just a smile and a nod. Later, when I was alone, I devoted myself to looking up facts on the Internet so that my ignorance wouldn't be so obvious. I've never been an idiot, really, and if it weren't for that English teacher I seduced in the ninth grade, perhaps I would have been a model kid, since I liked studying and spent hours and hours consulting Wikipedia and Encarta and a variety of digital newspapers and magazines, all to ensnare Margaret. Mía, the little Chilean woman, was a great help in this.

She knew a lot about American and even European literature; we would go to New York and look in used bookstores there. Sometimes I felt like staying in the Big Apple with Mía and forgetting all about provincial Louisville and Margaret the skinny *motorista,* but that woman had become a challenge. She knew I was a widower, of an older woman like her, also American, and coincidentally also a bleached blonde. That seemed strange to her. Honestly, it would have seemed strange to me, too.

BERTA

My love for Prince drained like water when you remove the plug from the sink, and the three of us could sit on the same bench in the Prado. Prince would sit between the two of us, and Araceli would caress my right hand without him noticing. At the time, Prince had already sold the motor scooter he'd inherited from Gringo, so we would go back to the neighborhood together after. He was still beautiful, although he didn't seem as delicate as before and didn't have his brother's animal attractiveness. He looked like a model since he wore the clothes that Johannes's foreign boyfriend used to give him. He always went around with a blue notebook that had his poems in it, but also the drafts of his sermons, and some homework assignment or other. Araceli, meanwhile, used a sophisticated notebook that zipped up, on which she had carefully inscribed the word POETRY in all caps. I also had a notebook solely for my writing. I don't know what could have happened to Prince's poems. If I see Johannes again one of these days, I'll ask her. At the time, they seemed good to me, and daring, not for their form, which was rather conventional, but for their ideas. At the workshop, we three also sat together, so some smart aleck gave us the nickname the Punta Gotica Crew. Since they didn't know Prince was Arturo Stuart's son, they would talk about the cathedral and the crazy man who'd thought of building it, and how the authorities were even crazier to allow it. Prince didn't say anything. He used to laugh. He had even white teeth and his hands . . . I've never again seen a man with hands like that, beautiful with delicate, long fingers. They made you want their caress. *Could he be homosexual or does he not like people of his own race?* I would think, trying to catch his eye, since I knew I was pretty and, since Araceli and I still had gold left, we dressed well.

I saw the dead man again yesterday. Aramís showed up in my apartment in Old Havana and told me I should move, since a hurricane was coming. He hadn't changed at all. He was still the same naked white guy, and the wound on his neck still bled.

"So when will I meet the love of my life?" I asked.

"Man or woman?" Aramís said with that sad irony of the dead, and I understood that he couldn't forgive that Araceli and I had been lovers.

"The gender doesn't matter," I told him, "but I want to be truly loved, to be loved like she loved me."

"But it didn't last."

"Nothing lasts."

"They killed the man who took my life," he said suddenly. "He wanted to come see you, but I didn't know if you'd consent."

"Gringo was executed?"

"His appeals ran out, first the governor of Texas, then the

147

Supreme Court said no; he took it badly, but he wants to know if he can come see you."

"Gringo is a dark soul and I don't want him near me . . . I need brightness, your brightness." Then I said to Aramís for the hundredth time, "Forgive me for what happened between Araceli and me, it was something we couldn't avoid. The thing is, Cuban men were hell to deal with, none of them were affectionate with us, they all wanted the same thing, to stick their dick in you and that's it; we got tired, we needed affection, the real kind, not pretend, so forgive me, Aramís, and rise up, ascend at last to the sidereal regions where the luminous beings like yourself await, don't let yourself get tangled up in the trash that took your life, stay away from Gringo."

"I can't," he said. "I try to rise, but something prevents me, it keeps me here hovering over the ground like a fumigation biplane. It's that I'm in an Nganga. Gringo told me so. 'I was bad, Aramís,' he told me. 'I couldn't just kill you and sell your meat, I gave your skull and bones to my *Padrino* in Palo, he's the old gray-haired guy keeping you as a slave, who forces you to do things that you don't remember later.'"

"I know who he is," I told him, "and I'm going to save you so you can rise up."

"Thank you, Berta," Aramís said, and was erased like a drop of water falling into water.

Last year, three people from the Mecenas publishing house came here, to Havana, to commission from me an anthology of Cienfuegos poets born after '59. I would have liked to decline the honor, but I needed the money, so I signed the contract and got to work. They didn't agree to include Prince. *He doesn't seem representative; after all, he was born in Camagüey,* they reasoned at first. *What about Michel Martín? Or Edel, the thin one, Pereira? Or Ian? Cienfuegos poets, really from Cienfuegos. Jesús Candelario*, I suggested to them, and then they claimed they didn't think it was appropriate to include Prince. *He's a monster*, they said, *including him would be a disservice to the poetry of Cienfuegos. It's enough that we've got that eyesore of a temple his father built in Punta Gotica.*

They did include Araceli.

GRINGO

I had to leave Mía because something in her triggered too much in me, her smooth skin filled me with bad desires, made me want to kill her; for nothing, Mía didn't have a dime, but I wanted to eat steaks made out of her, and that scared me. It's one thing to do something in the struggle to get ahead, and another thing entirely to become a filthy pervert who can't be with a woman unless it's to ingest her with a side of fries. The day I told her we should end it, she got depressed and was on the verge of moving me with her tears.

"It's because of that old whore."

"Yes, it's because of her." I told Mía to go to hell.

The dead were inciting me to eat Mía, especially the *guajira* Amarilis, because like a fool I still kept a piece of her skull and her other bones in the safe of my apartment in Louisville.

ROGELIO

Now they say to me, *You gave that up, the possibility of becoming a genius, like maestro Gaudí*, and I reply, *Yes, I gave it up*, but then, I think, you're born a genius. If it had been in my destiny to finish this, the cathedral of evil, it would be done; besides, I never aimed to be a genius, I always wanted to be one of those anonymous beings you see sitting in the park reading the paper and later don't remember having seen, I wanted to be one of those people, that's all. It's what I am now and I don't regret it; it's true that sometimes I take my bicycle, although my wife shouts at me, *Rogelio, remember your prostate, you're going to kill yourself, please,* I go over to Punta Gotica and stand staring at the ruins of what could have been my cathedral, a badge of honor, if you will. I close my eyes and think that things could have been different. Now, when the University of Cienfuegos finally has a department of Architecture and Civil Engineering, the dean, who studied with me in Santa Clara, sometimes invites me to give a lecture. "So you can earn a few pesos," he says condescendingly, affably, lording it over me. When I'm in front of the students, I start talking about Cuban architecture from the year 2000 to now, anxious and simultaneously wanting them to inquire, to ask about the cathedral, and perhaps at last a hand is raised and some young woman is interested:

"And how would we define the Black Cathedral, *profe*?"

"As madness, genius, or both?" some other young person asks.

I expand. I practically make a compendium of the history of architecture, I go back to the Mayas, mention the Assyrians, then I jump and I'm already in the early European Middle Ages, and they look at me, knowing I am being evasive, that I'm afraid to respond.

"I gave up being great," I tell my brother Felipe when

we're both drunk. "I gave up being great although an angel showed me the path; it was an angel without wings, so I should have always suspected it was an evil angel, a demon."

"Don't get depressed." My brother studied psychology but didn't finish his degree, and every day he has to go work as a bookkeeper at one of those little dime-a-dozen food-supply companies, until he retires like me. I'm already retired, and although I spent thirty years working as an architect, my pension isn't enough to cover anything, I have to draw up some little plan for any old builder to more or less get by. To think that when we were Sacramentalists, Arturo Stuart paid me two hundred pesos a day to build his church.

"Yes, but it was the evil cathedral," my brother repeats what I myself have told him hundreds of times. "So don't get depressed."

"The hell with the evil cathedral," I say. "Look at the state my house is in, it's falling apart."

I should have gone to Europe when I was young, or to the U.S., everything is there. There they still build on a large scale, individual-led architecture still exists there, not like here where everything comes in a Chinese, Brazilian, or Indian catalog, and you can't do a thing about it.

"Don't get depressed, let's talk about baseball." My brother sighs and takes one of those long sips that only old men take when they're already drunk.

GRINGO

She was older, but had something delicate and classy about her. The first time we slept together, she taught me how to remove her carbon-fiber-and-plastic leg, then she disrobed, and naked, she was much better. She was no hag, she had fifty-seven years under her belt, but they'd been put to good use. As I fucked her, I looked at that robotic leg that had been left on a shelf, and it was like looking at a strange alien gadget, that turned me on. I also liked racing on those Ducatis, the best thing Italy has given the world since the Renaissance, better even than her Harley-Davidson, which was a classic and all, but too heavy.

I thought she'd never ask me, but after spending nearly a year together, two days before my thirty-first birthday, Margaret asked me to come live at her house, just like that, simply, the way she did almost everything, as if she were the man. Then she noted that she had consulted her *Padrino* in Candomblé, and he had said I was the right man. *What a fucked-up* Padrino, I thought, and I acted as if I were praying for a while so she wouldn't notice anything.

GUTS

Acting like Arturo Stuart was going to let go of his cash as if he was another black-market pizza vendor, that was El Ruso's mistake, and on that September afternoon, when Antón Abramovich sent me and Gordo Gris to get the money, the end of his empire began.

GRINGO

We were too visible, even for this country full of outlandish people: a fiftysomething with hair so pale it looked white, who dressed all in black leather, and a young, thin black man wearing Armani, both on a pair of supermodern motorcycles, crisscrossing the county's local roads at high speed, were attention-grabbing as all hell, and Margaret and I often heard the beeping of patrol cars demanding that we pull over because we were going over the speed limit. We found it funny, all that heat from the police, and sometimes I played *el niche*: playing *el niche* was to talk with a pronounced accent, to get a laugh out of it. I liked that about her, she was always ready for a joke or a fight. So many times, I had to fight guys who had looked at her with pity or had offended her in some way. She would jump on them and hit them, that was really something because in the *Yuma*, any old weakling is over two hundred pounds of muscle, and at my heaviest, I've never weighed more than a hundred and eighty, so I was forced to act quickly and directly, always aiming at the chin. Always willing to take out my gun, too, just in case. Sometimes she and I came out losing, but seldom.

I liked that about my old lady Margaret; what I didn't like was her playing at politics and thinking so much about the poor only to go and drink a five-hundred-dollar bottle of Chivas Regal.

IAN RODRÍGUEZ, *Cienfuegos poet and writer*

I met the Deacon on a day that looked like rain, so few people came to the workshop because of that. Araceli and Berta brought him. I recall that when I asked him about his literary preferences (I usually interrogate everyone who is starting, to confirm their reading background), he talked to me about William Carlos Williams and Wallace Stevens, poets he was quite dedicated to at the time, although later his manner of understanding poetry had little to do with the work of those American authors. When I stop to think about it, the Deacon's poetry was similar to that of Rimbaud and San Juan de la Cruz. Perhaps peppered with a tendency toward the postmodern, which suited him. When he joined the workshop, he already had a few things written, with the mistakes you'd expect to find with a beginner, but not bad at all. Many poets with published books would have envied that stack of poems written in a notebook, scrawled quickly by hand, like a trail of ants. That's why I would say to him, *I don't understand that, read it to me*, and he would raise his clear, virile voice that contrasted so sharply with his thin body and its fragile appearance.

He was a natural. He had been born with poetic instinct and was all over the place; sometimes that conspired against the harmony of much of his work. I would say to him, "Inspiration is a wild horse, you can't allow it to always run free, at the right moment, you have to tame it." He agreed with me, but taming that tendency toward psychic automatism was difficult for him. Even in the book that ended up receiving the Pinos Nuevos prize, in some poems you can see that accelerated lyricism.

He always came to the workshop in the company of those two girls. The relationship between them seemed to be beyond mere literary camaraderie. I was sure that they were lovers, and I thought that the Deacon was lucky since the young women were very pretty.

Of the two of them, although she was lazy about writing poetry, leaning more toward reading and contemplation, Araceli was the more gifted. She liked hendecasyllables, and her sonnets were rather good, but they didn't seem like they were written by someone so young. Berta, on the other hand, worked hard on some long, free-verse poems, laborious and stylized, but I always saw that the narrative form was a better fit for her, to be honest. Now that she is such a well-known novelist, when she comes to Cienfuegos on some Casa de las Américas jury or something like that, I recall how sad she got when I recommended she go see Marcial, the one with the bike, or to make the most of Atilio's being in Cienfuegos, and talk to one of those two. "But I don't have anything written in prose, what am I going to show them? My tits?" she replied with that hint of sarcasm that could be a bit tiring at times, and that characterized the three of them, especially the Deacon, which I forgave him because I sensed his need to protect himself from society. Many looked down on them because, as I already said, they acted as if they were a trio of lovers. When they came into the bookstore here where I lead the workshop, the employees kept looking at them and went on and on about how *that white chick from Santiespíritu landed in Cienfuegos out of nowhere and the little* mulata *let her stay at her house, and who brings someone into your home if it's not out of interest, sexual in this case?* And that *the Deacon, son of that crazy pastor from Punta Gotica who has spent years and years making a cathedral that's never finished, and it's so big that one day we're going to be able to see it from the bookstore doorway without having to raise our heads, he's also in the middle of it and fucking them both, although the* mulata *might not know he's also with the other one, because when she doesn't come to the workshop because of x or y, look how that little white girl grabs on to the Deacon's arm, and when class is over, they don't go to Punta Gotica, but go up the Boulevard, and one day, I saw them go into one of those love hotels where people only go to fuck.*

That's what I heard people saying about them, the times that I was looking for some book or another and was by the bookshelves without them noticing.

GRINGO

Sometimes you have to kill someone even if you don't want to, it's something that eats away at you, a *disjunctive*, as they say; that happened to me with Margaret, my second wife, I would have wanted to spend my whole life with her, but in Louisville, that infamous small town, the game was starting to sour for me. Some people knew me, ranchers who'd seen me with Elsa, who wouldn't like to see me marry another old American woman, so I told Margaret that we should move to the Big Apple or at least Chicago, because I was a bit sick of the blue prairies and of horses, but she wouldn't agree. She felt like the alpha female.

"My life is here, darling," she said, then corrected herself. "Our life."

Fuck, I thought, *I have to lift something off her and get far away, I can't end up a widower twice over, because these Americans aren't as dumb as they seem at first.*

Besides, I'd grown to feel affection for her, and a guy like me can't afford the luxury of loving someone as sharp as Margaret, who, deep down, didn't love anyone. All you had to do was look at the surveillance cameras she had installed to watch the shop's employees, and how poorly she treated them at those meetings she sometimes asked me to attend.

There's no such thing as a good cripple, I would think, watching her act as if she was God's own cousin, thinking so highly of herself because she stayed thin while most women her age were a mass of pudding.

What convinced me was running into another black guy just like me. One day, I'm about to get into my Ferrari when I notice I'm being watched with hostility. I turn around, and a *mulato* with light eyes who was more or less my size, and with an accent laden with *r*'s that I disliked from the start, said to me, "You and I need to talk."

He was Pierre Giscard and he had been my old lady's lover, according to what he told me when we were sitting at a Starbucks with our espressos in front of us.

He spoke like a gigolo, a guy who thinks he can get anyone to do anything. He had just come back from Toronto, where he'd been sent to train a racing team, and he had just found out the news: Margaret O'Sullivan was now spoken for. I listened to him with the hint of a smile on my face, without taking him too seriously, but suddenly he said his money was running out and that he'd been investigating me and knew something about the strange death of my former wife, and I really didn't like that.

"I'll give you something," I said to him, "so you'll keep quiet." I said to him, "How much?" And I took out my checkbook and pen.

He shook his head.

"Do you accept cash?" I asked, playing along, but I had already decided to bump him off, and the total prick told me that, no, what he wanted was for me to leave Margaret alone, she wasn't the woman for me, and the proof was that they had continued to see each other, and if I didn't believe it, he had videos of it.

"Well," I said. "You win . . . You're Haitian, right?"

"French," he said arrogantly. "I'm not Caribbean like you . . . Leave now, while you can. I have a whole file I'll give to the police, so you know."

Then he stood up and the son of a bitch dared to hold out his hand to me. I shook it and smiled.

When he left, I got in the Ferrari and turned on the computer in the car. I went on the Internet and Google described Pierre Giscard as a former Formula One champion who, following an accident, was left with a head injury that caused erratic behavior and kept him from driving race cars.

He was a fool. If he had been the slightest bit sharper, he would have realized he couldn't take me on. Perhaps then he and Margaret would be alive, but he made a mistake, he thought I was a guy like him, the kind who trusts in laws and lawyers. That night, when we had just gone to bed, I asked Margaret if she knew a certain Pierre, and she got tense. She avoided my gaze when she said he was a friend, that was all, an unhappy kid who was as wounded as she was, even though you couldn't tell.

She's up to something, I told myself.

I spent three weeks watching the guy. I became an expert on him. I came to know where he lived and what his habits were. He didn't have friends, except for another Frenchman, a chef at one of the city's most exclusive restaurants, and Margaret, my wife, whom he usually visited when he assumed I wasn't home. I also avoided running into him. It only happened once, at the same Starbucks, and I told him that, yes, I was leaving, but he had to give me some time to get my affairs in order. The guy believed it, sighed loudly, and again shook my hand with his—thin, muscled, but lacking in energy. It was like shaking a dead bird.

"All clear, then?" he had the gall to ask.

"Yes," I said to him. "Don't say anything to Margaret. I don't want her to hate me."

"Okay." He smiled.

I spent a whole week wondering how I would enter his home. Coincidence helped me. One day, I discovered that the guy hid his key under the welcome mat so a Colombian maid called Lourdes could come in and clean. The maid went every other day: Monday, Wednesday, Friday, and Sunday. The other days, this Giscard had the key with him. The Colombian got there around nine in the morning. I took a risk. I prayed that no neighbor would see me, got to the front door of the Frenchman's house, lifted the mat, and copied the key on a piece of clay I'd bought at a toy store for kids. The next day, I took a bus to New York. On a Brooklyn street, I found a Puerto Rican locksmith. Everything else was easy. On a Tuesday, at three in the afternoon, I entered Giscard's residence. I put a silencer on my .45 and waited for him on the sofa. He took about two hours, but I finally heard some light steps, at first, then the key entering the lock. He opened the door. He put his briefcase on the steel-and-glass table, then lifted his head and saw me. He managed to take off his glasses. I didn't let him speak. I shot him in the face. I didn't do it out of revenge, I even liked him, he was a classy guy like me and had a way of carrying himself that reminded me of Prince, but one of us was enough.

I opened his closets and dressed in one of his track suits, all Nike, branded all the way down to the drawstring. I covered my head with an authentic Yankees cap. I put my own suit in a backpack. Then I took the keys to his car, a new Volvo. I put the corpse first in a plastic bag, then in an enormous black suitcase I'd brought with me. I went down the stairs with that suitcase and shoved the deceased in the trunk of the Volvo.

I went back to the dead man's home. I turned on the laptop I'd found on the table. I opened a Word document and wrote out a plot to murder Margaret O'Sullivan for being a slut and a bitch, and Ricardo Mora, alias Richard, for taking advantage of her.

BERTA

We played with words, I now recall; we pronounced one and it was like the syllables stayed in the air until we said more, and then they popped like soap bubbles. We played with words. *It's a way of approaching the poetic*, Ian the teacher would say, and we, Araceli and I, would take the words to the dock facing the sea, the part of Cienfuegos we liked most, and continue the game there. *Lapis lazuli*, I would say, and Araceli would respond with the word *transparency*. We played with words, and sometimes Prince came with us, but he didn't play. The sea seemed to be enough for him. He would go mute looking off into the distance, he would seem old, an old age that transcended us, an ancestral old age. He wasn't happy, perhaps that is why his poems were so good. We were happy. We couldn't help being happy. We were in love and my mother was starting to realize it. "Wouldn't it be better," she would say, "if Araceli started looking for her own place to live already? The two of you spend a lot of time together."

We played with words.

GRINGO

I killed her the following morning, I recall that a light rain was falling, the harbinger of fall. I already had in hand the passport and driver's license that claimed my name was Albert Rodríguez, an American citizen of Costa Rican origins. Those papers had cost me sixty thousand dollars, but they were of such good quality that I was able to use them to buy the .45 with which I did away with first Giscard and then my wife. I let her die doing what she liked so much, riding her perfect Harley-Davidson. I was on the Ducati. We stopped at an intersection for a stoplight. I was a few inches behind her. I took out the gun.

"Goodbye, my love," I whispered, and shot at the base of her skull. I didn't care about the traffic cameras at every stoplight in this country. I saw her fall over like a bird, and I took off without waiting for the green light. In my backpack, I had exactly $750,000 that I'd taken out of the safe.

I put away the motorcycle she'd given me for my birthday and the .45 in a barn on the outskirts of the city. Pierre Giscard's corpse was already there. I set the barn on fire, but beforehand, I took the guy's Volvo out, and as I drove it, I said goodbye forever to Louisville and to Ricardo Mora, alias Gringo. Or so I thought.

When I was young, I looked like Prince Andrew, small in stature and good-looking. I've never had a belly or a jiggly body, but back then I had the body of an ephebe in classical Greece. I'm from Tula, where the best weapons were made in the time of the czars, and where the great Leo Tolstoy is buried. My father was a professor in Tula University's History Department, but during the Great War, he fraternized with an American friend who loved archaeology and everything medieval. The conflict ended, and my old man and the American made the mistake of continuing to exchange letters, and that wasn't good at all for the Soviets. My papa was expelled from his chair at the university and was this close to being sent off for a spell in Siberia. Fortunately, Stalin died, and my father moved to Ukraine. The five of us moved into a building on the outskirts of Kiev: my parents, my two sisters, and me, when I was only five years old. At eighteen, I wanted to be a pilot, but it wasn't meant to be. With a father like mine, the authorities didn't think it appropriate to lend me one of their planes—*The best in the world*, they would say. I had to settle for industrial engineering. Since then, I promised myself not to ever place my trust in any state again. *I'm going to make money*, I told myself.

I got to Cienfuegos in the eighties, seven years after graduating, surrounded by other *bolos*, most of them Russian, but there were also Ukrainians, Moldavians, Byelorussians, Kazakhs, Armenians, and everything else. I learned everything here, to bathe regularly, to use deodorant, to truly enjoy a woman, and, something important: I learned that you can't be afraid. *If you're afraid, buy a dog*, as the Cubans say. Here, I confirmed something I'd already suspected: that I'm black. I suspected it because from a young age I liked jazz, the blues, salsa, and when I came to know the black woman, I fell hard and married Margarita, an English-literature student. My Queen Margot, I would call her. Things were going well for us because I was paid in rubles. Money was made to fill my pockets. Later, the Soviet Union turned to dust, my father died, and three years on, my mother also died. I stayed in Cuba and reaffirmed my purpose of becoming someone, *un negro ruso de salir*, as the Cubans say. Then, when I already had my bar, which drew the most select clientele from Europe, Canada, Mexico, Argentina, and Brazil, anxious to enjoy all kinds of sexual perversions in good company, I met Yusimí, a black girl with Indian features, with long hair, green eyes, tall, thin waisted, and with a nicely shaped behind. Her own aunt, a woman called Maribel, introduced her to me.

"Look," Maribel said to me. "The girl came from Guantánamo and has a really bad situation at home, she's willing to do anything as long as she can make a buck."

"Anything? Let me try her." That was my mistake, I went to bed with Yusimí, who was only fifteen years old then, and I wasn't able to be true to myself and buy her a house and reserve her for my personal use; no, I gave her to the dogs, human ones as well as ones on four legs, I got a lot of money out of her, but it hurt me when someone touched her. It hurt me as if someone was putting needles under my fingernails. It hurt me, but the money, the *dinero*, the bucks, the dough, the kopecks, the lettuce, the *pesetas*, the drachmas, the kroner, these are everything in life, the only thing you can believe in. Falling in love is shit; if Yusimí hadn't bewitched me, I wouldn't have wasted time messing with the Sacramentalists, I would have left that old madman Stuart alone, but I wanted to prove something, I needed to. I needed to prove to Yusimí that I was an alpha male, that here in Punta Gotica not even a leaf moved without my permission, and I ruined myself.

GRINGO

Five days later, they were talking on CNN about the extermination of Margaret O'Sullivan, former world motorcycling champion, first woman to participate in the Casablanca–Rabat rally, and of her good-looking husband, the Cuban-born athlete Ricardo Mora, dead under circumstances that had yet to be clarified, because while Margaret O'Sullivan had been finished off by a shot to the head while riding her Harley-Davidson, the charred corpse of Ricardo Mora was found in a stable on the outskirts of Louisville. Said barn had been deliberately burned down. Supposedly, the police possessed a recording from a traffic camera. Said recording implicated a certain young man of Brazilian origins turned French national, Pierre Giscard, who had been going out with Margaret O'Sullivan before she met Ricardo Mora. The police hadn't been able to find Giscard, who hadn't returned to his apartment since the night of the events. Ricardo Mora was the owner of a Ducati, a gift from the deceased, and the remains of a motorcycle were also found at the stable, besides the tire marks left by a pickup truck. But what most implicated the aforementioned Giscard was a murderous plot found on the hard drive of his laptop.

All this I heard and watched as I drank a Cuba Libre, lying in bed in a Hilton in Chicago.

El Ruso made a mistake, I think now as I stroll down Las Ramblas, a mistake, but he was like that, especially if Yusimí with the green eyes was nearby. He had to show off.

"Go back," he said to us, "and tell him that Antón Abramovich doesn't talk to the same person three times."

It was a mistake, but since Yusimí was looking at him with those eyes of hers that were as vacant as her head, had her legs crossed so you could see the edge of her panties, and was also caressing that Alaskan husky he'd brought himself from Russia, you couldn't say to him, *Listen, Ruso, you're making a mistake*, because he'd replace you quick as a rocket. So Gordo Gris and I drank the cognac remaining in our glasses, stood up, and went to see Arturo Stuart, knowing it was a mistake of the most serious kind, the kind you can't easily recover from. Arturo Stuart had connections, real connections: with the American church, with the Cuban government, and God knows who else, and the Sacramentalists in Cienfuegos numbered more than twenty thousand and were fanatics. Besides, Stuart was fearless, a black man of steel, and although he was courteous to us the first time, he was clear: "I don't want to see you around here again. Please, tell Antón Abramovich to try to build his synagogue, we'll know what to do." Abramovich didn't at all like that Stuart was calling him Jewish. "That fucking black bastard," he said, and Yusimí was present, so he repeated, "Go see Stuart, but go prepared," and Gordo Gris and I went to *la cuartería* where Arturo Stuart still lived with his wife, his younger son, Prince, and his only daughter, Johannes, when she came back from the ISA.

You're forced not to leave any loose ends, you have no choice. I had been living in Chicago for two years when I hear a woman's voice drop:

"Ricardo Mora Gutiérrez."

I had just gotten out of the car and was in the parking lot of one of the city's main jewelers, where I'd gone to buy a Rolex. I turn around and there's Mía. This country is 3.8 million square miles big and she picked the same city as me.

She was dressed in a depressing way, a miniskirt and a red jacket that matched the garish color of her boots; in addition, she was wearing so much makeup on her mouth and around her eyes that it turned my stomach.

"Ricardo," she repeated, and hugged me. "Everyone in Louisville was sure you'd burned up, but I knew it wasn't like that . . . I knew you were alive."

"Are you working the streets?"

"Yeah, what do you want from me? Life is hard." She burst out laughing and crying at the same time. "You know? I'm offering myself for seventy dollars an hour, me, who once charged a thousand bucks for one night."

She was no longer the little mystic Chilean from her time in Louisville. Now she was skinny and pale, she looked like death. It wasn't good for me to be seen with her, and I was about to brush her off, but then she told me that the police hadn't bought it, they'd interrogated everyone I knew, but she hadn't said anything.

"Are you using?" I asked.

"Yes. Angel dust."

"Why didn't you go back to Chile?"

"Nobody wants me in Santiago, I wrote to my older brother and he said that if I went there, he'd kill me . . . They found out I was a whore here. Berenice wrote to them."

Berenice was her cousin, a fat little woman who didn't look anything like Mía and worked as a nurse.

"So what did you do?"

"Nothing, he was right, I'm a whore . . . Please buy me a coffee."

Mía started crying, she was really down. I took her to my house and gave her five hundred dollars. She wanted to pay me in sex; I didn't want to, but I gave her some advice.

"Get lost, leave Chicago, and don't tell anyone you saw me."

But she didn't leave. Two weeks went by and on a rainy Thursday when I was coming back to my house, I noticed someone sitting on one of the steps to the front door. It was her.

It was spring, but in Chicago, it was cold out; in addition, she was wet, she smelled like vomit and cheap-whore sweat.

"Come in," I said, and she sat down on my new sofa, without any concern for her wet clothes.

I wouldn't have wanted to harm her, really, but in the U.S., there are 300 million inhabitants and when you've just arrived, you think it's easy to get lost, but it's not like that, everything is tracked here, and the papers I had in Albert Rodríguez's name had cost me a lot and I wasn't willing to lose it all because of a junkie like Mía, who was surely going to talk about me, if not right away, then when she was high. I had to do it, I liked her and she was a very good fuck, but it was her or me. I had no choice.

167

"How did you get so low?" I asked, when I served her some coffee, and she told me that after I'd left her, she met an artist, a painter from Soho who was a poet like her, and they'd gone to Peru together and had climbed up to Machu Picchu, but the painter had gone mad. She didn't share any more details, only added that this guy had stolen more than ten grand in jewelry and had purchased a painting under the impression that it was van Gogh's *Sunflowers*.

"Have you told anyone about me?"

"Of course not, Ricardo," she said. "Besides, here in Chicago, I only have you; I don't know why, but now customers run away from me, me, who used to charge a thousand dollars a night."

"Didn't I tell you to leave the city?"

"Yes, but where was I going to go, Ricardo, with your filthy five hundred dollars?"

"Don't call me Ricardo anymore, use Mauricio."

"Okay, you'll be Mauricio," she said. "Did you really kill her? The witch, I mean."

"No. I just don't want any trouble."

"You don't have anything to fear with me."

"Of course not, you're my little Araucan princess."

I stood up from the armchair and sat on the sofa with her. First, I took her right hand and brought it to my lips, then I caressed her cheeks; she purred like a kitten, then I moved on to her neck and squeezed it until she died, with barely a moan. I buried her in the yard. I was sure no one had seen her. My block is quiet. Nonetheless, I later learned there was a witness: an old American woman saw me go inside with a very thin woman and later saw me burying a large heap in my yard, but she didn't say anything, she didn't want any trouble, I think.

I moved to Portland.

MARIANO MESA GUILLOT

The intelligent one was the other one, the younger one, Prince, so I wasn't surprised at all when at only seventeen, he won the Pinos Nuevos prize for poetry, and one day, my wife and I saw him on television, sitting across from the newscaster Raquel Mayedo to answer questions as if he were a movie star. He was much taller, at least six foot three, but he still had that angel's face he'd always had and seemed less nervous even than the newscaster, as if he'd been born for the camera and knew it. He read one of his poems, it was about the only subject that he had ever found interesting, death. His voice sounded clear and virile. The voice of a preacher of lies. The voice of someone as false as a wooden nickel. "He's evil," I told my wife, "he may be promising, but he's evil." I don't want to come across as an oracle now, but you could tell, I said it without knowing how evil he could be. I'm sure that the other kid was just a victim of circumstance. To have such a terrible illness while so young must alter anyone's brain.

But who am I to judge anyone? I'm a rather mad old man who spent his life trying to cultivate the young, without success. What's true is that when someone talks to me about that, about the *new man*, I want to scream. The efforts other educators and I made were enormous, and they practically all turned out bad. Even the good ones aren't like we expected.

I would call them *the Black Cathedral generation*, if you asked me. Look at Berta, a kid with a talent for words who carried out her dream of becoming a writer. So what? She left her city. She lives in Havana, and that she's a native of Punta Gotica, the most modest neighborhood of Cienfuegos, barely figures into her novels. Regarding the others, Yohandris lives in Barcelona, the only thing he was good for was to bounce balls off his head during the intermunicipal soccer tournaments, and in the end, he turned out the best because he didn't go to prison and he helps his aging father financially. He sends him everything from over there, but he doesn't come to Cuba. Johannes, the only sane one among the Stuarts, is famous now and even shows up in contemporary art books, and according to gossip magazines, she just bought herself a little island in the Mediterranean. I'm sure she'll meet a bad end. That whole family is destined for a bad end. They're cursed; I don't like to use that word because I'm a materialist and I don't even believe in my own mother, but it's the truth, those people are cursed. Gringo, well, I'd rather not talk about him, but in the end they gave him a lethal injection. A good way to go for a murderer like that, but I knew him, I was his teacher and I still remember him. I remember his smile and how he was interested in math, and how he sang patriotic songs at school activities, how respectful he was, and how his mother, the late Clara, cared for him. All just to wind up with Salvador the Pig, selling human flesh to the whole neighborhood of Punta Gorda, making them so notorious as cannibals to the neighborhood's residents that even though years have gone by, when you say, "I'm from Punta Gotica," they give you a dirty look, and if they're daring enough, they say, "Ah, the cannibal neighborhood?" Nacho Fat-Lips, that one has spent his days in jail. He has his reputation, as he says, and when he gets out . . . well, he's about to get out, it has already been twenty-five years, and he's been locked up since he was a teenager. Bárbaro, my nephew, is lost, and not because of his homosexual condition, but because he goes around dressed like a woman at the age of forty-five and he throws up such a fuss over any little thing that you want to run and hide, like the child he never was. Something has happened to this generation, I don't know.

Was it worth it, all that effort to educate them? I thought that afternoon when Samuel Prince appeared on the TV with his brand-new book, published in Havana, in his hands. I even thought he was going to mention me: I was the principal of his school in his early years of developing as a poet. If not for me, his teachers wouldn't have authorized him to go to the province library to read during school hours, but he didn't mention me. Instead, when they asked him about his influences, between Ezra Pound, T. S. Eliot, Lezama, Rimbaud, and Valéry, he named a Pablo, who was his Palo *Padrino*. That big black guy with a hundred beaded necklaces who could unleash evil all by himself.

GRINGO

I shouldn't have gone back to Texas. But on one of those days when you can't be outside in Portland even with three coats on, and you go out to shovel the snow and clear the door, Lucy said to me, "Let's go to Dallas, there's a fair with auto parts from all over the country, from fucking Mexico, and you can find wonders."

Of all the women I met in this country, including Nadine the Indian terrorist, Lucy was my favorite, although the bitch, after she found out all about me, she left me and divorced me through her lawyers. She never faced me again, but I have to admit that there was something about her, she was *mulata*, short, thin, with a nice ass, and she didn't look American. She was always jumping from side to side as if she had springs instead of bones. Sometimes she used to worry about where I got my money, but at a certain point, when we had just screwed and were still in bed, I had to tell her I was a secret agent, that I was telling her because I trusted her and she shouldn't share that information with anyone.

"Something like Bond," she said, and hugged me tight because even though we had the heat on, she was always cold and wanting to fuck. She fucked more than Cuban women and was nasty in bed. She learned each and every perversion she found in those ladies' magazines and later applied them to me. *Do this to me*, she would say, and then, *Do that*. I loved to please her, and I thought that since Johannes was never going to be mine, Lucy wasn't a bad option. I had married her, not to take all her dough, but because I needed to be with someone who seemed like she was from over there, from Cuba. She was the daughter of a doctor of Jamaican origins, who had fought in the Vietnam War like fucking Colin Powell, and of a Greek woman, much younger than him. Lucy was the closest thing to any little *mulata* walking around Cienfuegos looking for someone to stick it in her. I liked the old Jamaican man, he played basketball well enough, and although he was religious, evangelical, he wasn't as caught up in all that bullshit as the Christians in Cuba, who spend all day spouting idiocy and thinking they know the divine will. I am sure that's not how it is, because if anyone knows his will, then God must be an absolute moron. If I knew his will, I would have done better to go to New York on a trip, and not what Lucy and I did, which was pack up the back of the Ford pickup and drive to Texas, without knowing that in that damn state of cowboys, Indians, and Mexicans, an FBI agent, Robert Smith, one of those guys with an insatiable lust for resolving cold cases, was looking for me. He was looking for me because of what happened to Elsa and what happened to Margaret, he had subordinates asking around in Dallas, Houston, Austin, San Antonio, Waco, and in Kentucky itself. Not satisfied with this, he had put a photo on the Internet in which I appeared with Elsa's children, all of us happy, standing at the bar at Blue Bird ranch. If I had obeyed my instincts, I wouldn't have gone back to Texas even by force.

We spent a week getting there because we had money. I had twenty-four thousand dollars in cash, and Lucy's generous father, convinced of his daughter's uselessness, lent her his Gold MasterCard.

It went well for us along the way, we made the most of the network of small hotels for newlyweds that this country is full of and fucked like crazy. We were also drugged up, but no one noticed: Lucy graduated from a good college, and although she tried, she didn't talk like one of those crazy black girls. She spoke like a university graduate, the kind who are convinced they deserve everything, and sometimes I couldn't stand her petulance. But when we were in sync, it was bearable and even pleasing that my wife knew so much about books, art, and so much that was useless in the end, because she needed my help to so much as fry an egg. That, the thing about the books, was the only thing I liked about Lucy having gone to college. I still couldn't stand American TV, and as far as Latin TV goes, what a load of shit. Sometimes, I thought that that Carlitos Otero and the ass-faced blond presenter from *Caso Cerrado* had left their brains in lovely little Cuba. So I kept reading, struggling with books, even ones written in English. Lucy helped me to understand the secrets of prose. Sometimes I think that what I needed was time, that if they hadn't caught me so quickly, I would have made amends and would have stopped being Gringo, Satan, or the *diabolical predator* as the newspapers in Miami called me, and now I would truly be Albert Rodríguez, an exemplary citizen, a writer, by all accounts, because that was my dream, to start writing someday, to make more realistic stories than most of the others, that don't teach you anything about life. Another thing I could have been was a singer. That's what Lucy would say to me when we were driving. We went fast in my brand-new Ford. We would go a hundred miles an hour and I would sing a song by that Joaquín Sabina, who Berta liked so much. She listened to him all the time, I remember.

"*Querías hacer turismo al borde del abismo,*" I would sing.

"Translate it for me," Lucy would beg, "and look at the road or you're going to get us killed."

But the highways of this damn country are glorious, not like Cuba's, all full of potholes. I would think about the people in the neighborhood, and Berta. I would have married her if I'd had a different life, if it wasn't for that Johannes coming to fuck up my life.

You do sing very good, honey, Lucy would suddenly say, and I would smile, satisfied, and every once in a while, if we didn't see a patrol car nearby, we'd open the cooler and drink some beer, German or Dutch, as it should be. In sum, I was happily going a hundred miles an hour on a highway smooth as a calm sea without knowing that in Houston, Texas, an Indian Fed, apparently a Sioux, was asking around about me, putting together loose ends, finding clues, convinced that something wasn't right about the late Elsa Pound's Cuban widower.

My arrest was simple. When we were already in Texas, near a little town called Dalhart, we stopped at a gas station, and while Lucy went to the bathroom, I got out to stretch my legs. Then two police came up to me and asked for my identification. It was as if we were in Cuba, where it's normal for a policeman to see a black man and pounce on him with his claws out, saying, "*Carné de identidad.*"

Since I didn't look like an immigrant, my clothes were of the highest quality, and my new pickup truck exuded comfort and status, I understood that something dire was going on.

"What is wrong, officers?" I asked, trying to imbue my words with that liquid quality, without consonants, that I learned by hanging around with classy American women, and that without a doubt is a sign of distinction and good English.

It didn't do anything for me.

"Identification," the police demanded.

One of them was a Chicano of medium build, while the other one was a tall, strong redhead. They both had their hands close to their weapons. In addition, I was somewhat stoned and drunk, so my movements were slow and I wouldn't be able to act quickly enough. All that went through my brain while I leaned over and looked in the car's glove compartment for my driver's license with the name Albert Rodríguez on it.

The sun was starting to set, one of them looked at my documents while the other didn't stop watching me.

Then the Mexican said, "You have to come with us, Mr. Albert."

Lucy despaired when she saw them putting handcuffs on me. She thought I was being arrested for drug consumption and claimed she had connections in Chicago, since she was friends with the wife of the Democratic candidate for president, Barack Obama, and if they didn't let me go right then, she would make a scandal like they'd never seen . . . *There will be consequences.*

"We're saving your life, *señora* or *señorita*," the Chicano cop said in Spanish, mistaking Lucy for one more Latina, and she didn't understand a word.

"Don't you worry, my love," I said naïvely, thinking that everything could be fixed, since my *Padrino*'s dead and my own dead woman would know how to get me out of the jam. But when I got to Houston, the FBI agent Robert Smith was waiting for me. Evelyn, Elsa Pound's daughter, was with him.

She recognized me right away, of course, although I pretended it was the first time I'd seen her.

GUTS

He wasn't home. It was already six in the evening, and Prince told us that he must still be at the temple. I would have waited for him, but Gordo Gris said to me, "Let's go look for him there," and I said, "So let's go," and we went.

GRINGO

Did I become a hummingbird, or am I still waiting for these people I harmed so much to watch me die? In any event, when the lethal solution fills my veins, I'm going to go to Cienfuegos, I'm going to enter through its bay, I'll leave behind the neighborhood of Punta Gorda, the port, Martí Park, and I'll go back to where I was born, Punta Gotica, to be born again. I'm going to be born again and I'll try not to be a bad guy. I'll start as someone else. I'll start by asking forgiveness, first from Elsa, then Margaret, and finally Mía: three women who welcomed me in this cold country and who later I murdered. I'd also ask for forgiveness from Aramís, from the second *guajiro* whose name I never knew, and Amarilis. Perhaps I should go even further back and ask my mother for forgiveness for the pain of being born from her womb. Even ask God for forgiveness for not having allowed him to make me be born a bird or an insect or an inanimate rock. Ask everyone for forgiveness, ask that fat Billy Holden, who's carefully drying his tears because he doesn't want anyone to see that he's crying for me, for Satan, the murderer of women.

IBRAHIM

I saw those two representatives of the Leviathan on earth arrive, those two archdemons who thought they were something because they were armed. The *mulato* walked ahead, then came the fat one, who seemed like a sperm whale. They were coming to interrupt the Lord's work. They weren't able to perceive the host of angels surrounding us. Ignorant men. They arrived and addressed brother Arturo, and he lifted his hammer and brought it down on the head of the fat man, who fell, senseless, and then, looking into the *mulato*'s eyes, he said to him, "Pick up your companion and go in the name of the Lord."

"Amen," we all said.

The *mulato*, a young man with an unpronounceable name who everyone in the neighborhood knew as Guts, crouched down alongside the fat man and said that unfortunately that's not where things would end, that el Ruso would take the appropriate measures. We all began to laugh. We knew who el Ruso was, a creature worse than a pig's bite, but we weren't afraid of him, we were Sacramentalists, the keepers of Christ's shroud. Who then prevailed over us? No one but God.

GUTS

"Didn't I tell you I didn't want to see you around here anymore?" he said to us before we said anything, and he again broke one of the bricks with his small sledgehammer, adjusting it to the necessary size.

"You'll forgive us, Arturo," I said, "but el Ruso says—"

"El Ruso can kiss my ass and God's, you know?"

"Stop sucking so much cock, you fucking loon, fucking black monkey, what the fuck do I care about your God, *cojones*," Gordo Gris said.

The old man let him finish. He let him slap at him and get close enough to push him in the stomach, and for a moment he seemed to turn tiny, as if he'd become afraid of Gordo's three hundred pounds on his six-foot-two frame, but then he smiled.

"You're too fat for God and for me," he said, and went at him quickly with the hammer, so quickly that I was left stunned, and if I had time, actually, I'd go see what this Arturo Stuart did back in his Camagüey days, I would investigate, but I'm not going to leave Barcelona for lovely little Cuba to find out about the habits of a dead man. I saw Gordo Gris fall like a building coming down, and suddenly more than a thousand Sacramentalists were surrounding us, lifting their arms and singing hallelujahs, they were the same people who had always lived in the neighborhood, but now they weren't afraid of el Ruso, and less still of me. *I've got to get out of here*, I thought, and I already had a Catalan girlfriend, who passed herself off as a photographer and enjoyed taking pictures of me and had as her only demand "Shave your head, Yohandris *mío*."

"So I can look like a damn black tube of deodorant?" I would ask, and she would tell me, "Grow some dreadlocks," and I would say, "Enough, I'm not a fucking Rastafari," but I didn't explain that for my job with el Ruso, I had to look as normal and as elegant as possible.

PART THREE

NACHO FAT-LIPS

I had been in prison for ten years already when el Ruso sent me the message that a young man was coming to the Shark, the high-security ward here at Ariza, and that my job was to take care of him and I'd have everything squared away when I got out. *Who is it?* I asked the messenger, and when he said the name, I remembered Cricket and how we would do headers with soccer balls that we went to steal from Punta Gorda. Yes, I remembered, and I remembered how Guts and I peeped at his sister, Johannes, and at his mom, too, who was hot. It hurt me to think of my pal Guts. He had left for that Spain that's over in the Europes, in other words, far as fucking hell, without saying goodbye to me. Yes, I remembered, and even though I could give a shit about el Ruso—after all, whatever he was out there in the street, I was twice that here in the Shark—I said to tell him, "Okay, nothing will happen to your kid, who fucks *yumas* and little white chicks, nothing at all, don't worry . . . I already know he's in prison because of you." *The piece of shit*, I thought, because I don't do anyone's bidding. I know the number on the Cuban president's ID card, so how could I be afraid of anyone? "Let him come," I said to tell him, "nobody's going to touch him 'cause he was my childhood buddy, but he has to do everything I say for this to work, is that clear?"

"Yes, Nacho," the messenger said.

"Yes, Nacho what?"

"Yes, Nacho Fat-Lips." He looked at my lips with mistrust, as if he was afraid I was going to kiss him.

I've got to get respect.

He came the next day. He looked more like one of those Brazilian athletes who play for Real Madrid. His girlfriend from the Europes had supplied him with good stuff. He was smiling from ear to ear, he was tall and strong, a bodybuilder, used to eating meat every day and popping cherries whenever he felt like it, he didn't seem to realize that it was obligatory here to follow my rules, since without me, he was nothing. He thought he deserved respect. He laughed at Piggy, who was a *bugarrón* and all, but a tough guy who had been Gringo's pal, and Gringo is the only person I ever really respected and respect. Not because of his dead—after all, I've racked up more bodies than him—but because of how he looked at you.

If Gringo had been here, it's certain we would have had epic fights. We would've left a mark on this slave pit.

Cricket was nothing more than el Ruso's puppet. A guy who can only do another's bidding, I didn't like that.

When he said to me, "I'm going to inject myself with AIDS so I can make my way and have my sentence reduced, and show these guys I've got balls," I said to him, "Go on ahead, get to it, there's no use going backward."

I didn't think he was as crazy as all that.

You see every kind here; some inject petroleum into their own hand so the arm will rot and they can take a vacation in the hospital.

The ones who have AIDS sell infected needles, but the only people who buy them are just fools or they need to take revenge.

This kid, Cricket, was no regular fool. He had a chick from the Europes and was protected by el Ruso. In addition, his sentence was twelve years, and that time goes by quickly; besides, his sentence was sure to be reduced. He knew how to fight. He handed out some blows you could respect. One day, I egged on Piggy to try out Cricket, to see if he was a real man or a sewer rat.

"Piggy," I said to him, "if you keep letting Cricket get away from you, you're going to have to answer to me, even if you were Gringo's pal, so now you know . . ."

At shower time, Cricket had just entered the showers when Piggy jumped him with a fork.

"*Sala'o!*"

"Careful, Cricket!" somebody yelled.

He reacted quickly.

Just one punch and they had to pour water on Piggy's hooves to revive him. Cricket didn't kill him because he didn't want to. He stopped at pissing on his face. Of course, at bottom Piggy is a nobody, not even a useless piece of shit, and now, with Gringo dead, if Piggy were younger, I'd have him sucking my cock, but that punch made an impression. Piggy weighed about 280 pounds and it wasn't all fat.

To me, Cricket was crazy, and he missed black Yusimí, who he shared with el Ruso even though that European chick bribed the guards to come and see him, so much that he couldn't take it anymore and said to himself one day, *I have to get out of here*. Saying that kills a man little by little, it dries him up inside, leaves him soulless, turns him into a zombie. *I have to get out of here*, he said to himself, and that was the only way he saw to do it, how naïve, what an idiot. He didn't think that with AIDS, Yusimí wouldn't even look at him, not even in a picture. I know that Yusimí. I've seen nude photos of her and I don't know what others see in her. She's just a black girl with light-colored eyes, in good shape, that's true, but too skinny. That Yusimí was a real she-devil. More people are here, in prison, because of her than for attacking tourists. The first of all of them, Piggy, lost his money trying to fuck her and was left with blue balls, what madness. If I ever find myself out on the street—it's an expression, because I don't get any passes, I'm practically part of the furniture here—I'll go over to el Ruso's den to see what kind of woman she is. And I'll go to see the Black Cathedral.

SIMÓN ROGER DUEÑAS, *inmate*

I'm an example of how *not* to be in this life, a dreamer, that's why they did me in, for not being weak willed like so many people who follow along like sheep, for themselves, only for themselves—because I always wanted to share, to be a musketeer, a D'Artagnan of the Caribbean. Ever since I was in elementary school, I've been like that. I gave everything away from my snack to pencils, notebooks, everything, and they took advantage of me. Since I've always been this way, small and thin, my friends used me to climb in the principal's window to steal tests and student records. They used me. Another thing I've always been good at is dancing, it's a shame I've always been feminine, too much so for the art-school teachers, who, although the majority of them were as big of fairies as I was, didn't accept me, they said I lacked virility, and since I couldn't become a contemporary dancer, I wanted to be a choreographer, but I didn't have a good memory, and to be a choreographer you need a scary good memory, I would blank out on the choreography tests, and I had no other choice than to start working as a performer at the only cabaret in Cienfuegos that allowed a transvestite show. I was known as Edith Piaf at that show, not because I looked anything like the French diva, she was ugly as all hell, but because I always wear a sad face, even when I smile, I look sad, and that's because when I was still a child, my father died of cancer. That cabaret, El Costa Sur, was my point of no return. Foreigners like transvestites! And they liked me best of all, I've always been an admirer of good manners, and of history, because that's my truest interest, history, and if it's medieval European history, even better. Before all of my clothes were even off, I was already talking to them about Otto the Great, Pepin the Short, and Cnut the Great, the Danish conqueror of the British Isles. They were astonished as they listened to me. One of them was the one who gave me AIDS, an Austrian, by the looks of it, like Hitler, since then I can't stand Germanic types, I hope they lose every World Cup ever. Of course, when I think of it, it was my fault, I should have told him to put on a condom, that's pretty basic. But I've always had a weakness for those blonds, and this one with his shiny yellow hair and blue eyes fascinated me the minute I saw him. *He looks like Tristan*, I said to myself when he got out of the Nissan and came over to greet me in good Spanish, then asked me if I wanted to go for a spin.

"Of course," I said, and linked my arm with his.

We spent a marvelous six months together, he took me to Soroa, to the Viñales Valley, to Baracoa. I had never been to those places. He was jealous and insisted I leave the transvestite show, and when he went back to Austria, he sent a maid to help me, who also spied on me, then he would bring me first-rate clothing, fancy underwear and sophisticated dresses. Not that shit that whores wear, nothing like that. He also brought me history books, man, monographs about Frederick Barbarossa, Thomas Aquinas, Giotto, Paracelsus. I later had to sell all of that, books and dresses, because I was left without a cent when he started to change. He became like all men, a liar. He would say one thing to me, and then I would find out the opposite, and so on.

In the end, he broke up with me. He gave me AIDS and broke my heart. I'm in prison because of him, because when I found out he was maintaining another relationship in Punta Gorda, with one of those femmes who think they're somebody because their parents went to med school, I went to see her and made a scandal and pulled a knife on her, and I lost control and cut her cheek. I didn't do anything to her, it was just a scratch, but they sent me here anyway, to Ariza. Here, when they tested me, was when I found out I was infected, I spent three months in the infirmary, and they would have set me free, but things got complicated: the femme in the bed next to mine, to whom I had recounted my love story with the Austrian, ended up mocking me. When I finished telling him, he said I was just a pathetic whore and that it was all a lie, that I was too skinny and ugly for anyone to love me. *Shut up*, I warned him. But he went on and on. The nurse had forgotten a pair of scissors on the little metal table, and I lost control. I grabbed the scissors and stabbed the *maricón* in the throat. I really did behave poorly toward him. He was whispering, *Help me, Edith, help me*, but I was furious, so furious that I didn't even remove the scissors, and when the nurse came, the fairy had already died. So then I got twenty years, and here I am, in charge of the ward of homosexuals with AIDS. Nothing happens here without my consent, so when the so-called David King, better known as Cricket, needed an infected needle, he came to see me. I was sitting in the common area, in front of the TV set. There was an educational show on about the crusade of King Saint Louis, and no one was interested in it, so it was just me and another prisoner there.

I feel like I can still see him, an enormous kid, practically a giant, wearing expensive cologne, the kind you can barely get in Cuba, wearing, besides, a pair of those Adidas sneakers that cost more than a hundred dollars, that kids kill to have. He looked more like an athlete than a convict.

"Edith, I have to talk to you."

"Shoot."

"I need the stuff."

"For?"

"What do you mean 'for'?"

"Allow me to explain something to you about AIDS, *pimpollo*. HIV is divided into strains; there are stronger ones that are very dangerous, others are weaker, like a cold, those are the ideal ones if you want a long life, but they're harder to find. Months and months can go by before a lab detects you're sick. Do you want the stuff to give it to some guy as revenge, or to give it to yourself and spend a little vacation in the infirmary?"

"The second one."

"Okay, you need a strain like mine, which is pretty severe, but is quickly detected, and if you take the medication regularly, it's like a chronic illness, like diabetes or something like that . . . That'll be fifty dollars and ten cartons of cigarettes."

"Okay, when?"

"Tomorrow afternoon, but don't change your mind later."

"I won't change my mind." He stood by my side.

"What cologne is that?" I asked when he was already leaving.

"Chanel No. 5."

BERTA

All that is left of the Stuarts' time in Cienfuegos are the ruins of the cathedral, some early work or other of Johannes's, and Prince's poems. The mother went back to Camagüey, I think. She was the most innocent in this story, and the one who lost the most. A while ago, I was about to go see Prince at the psychiatric hospital. I called on the phone first.

"This is not only a hospital, but a penitentiary as well . . . This patient is a dangerous murderer, ma'am," the person who answered the phone said to me, after identifying herself as Dr. Ania Teresa Pereira.

I was about to ask her if Prince had changed much, if he was still a beautiful man, but I didn't. I only thanked her and hung up. Prince's illness is called hebephrenic schizophrenia. I know because I read it in a digital magazine about psychiatry published by the University of Havana. In short, Prince is crazy.

Am I crazy since I speak with ghosts and, at the age of thirty-five, I still dream of meeting the man or woman of my dreams? Am I crazy? I don't know. Prince thought that by sacrificing his parents, he would be able to save his brother, David King, from illness and death and acted accordingly. I don't know why he did it. Did he love his brother that much or did he hate Arturo Stuart and his wife to the extent that he would use this a pretext? I don't know, and I very much doubt I ever will, especially now that Cricket is dead and only Prince remains, locked up forever in a psych ward. Does it matter that much to know why we are so bad, so heartless and lacking in scruples? I don't know if it does, I can't answer my own question.

When it happened, Prince had just published his first book, and a piece had come out in the paper by a journalist given to rhetoric, who called him "the prince of Cienfuegos and Cuban poetry." I remember the reception they organized in his honor at the Union of Writers and Artists. He wore an elegant cream-colored suit, and never again as on that night did he look like Michael Jackson before he bleached his skin. They invited me to that dinner at the last minute. Araceli and I were no longer lovers, so I called Marcial, the prose writer, on the phone, and he agreed to accompany me. A half hour in, Araceli arrived, dressed all in white, in the company of an Argentine guy, a medical student. We looked at each other with hate, she and I, but we looked at each other, after all, and we looked at each other again when Prince started to read, since the poem was undoubtedly about us, it was something so moving that as I tell it now, I have to dry my eyes.

"Forget about her," Marcial said to me, and I appreciated that.

Prince seemed to have his whole life ahead of him at that moment, and I felt like my life was ending, and nonetheless, everything seemed so different, I think now, so fucking—irritatingly—different. Lucky for me, now I am here in Havana, living in an apartment that's not bad at all, although the dead man told me I have to move because it will soon collapse, I've won prizes and published books that I'm not completely satisfied with, but what am I going to do when I was born in Punta Gotica in a tiny little room and sometimes all my mother and I had was just one avocado to split between the two of us? *I'm alive*, I tell myself in the morning when I open up the balcony and look outside, at the people in La Víbora, who look like ants as they go to work. *I'm alive and I'll meet someone*, I tell myself, but first I'll go to that fucking Pablo's house, that damn Palero, and take Aramís's skull away from him so that Aramís can rise up and find the peace he so needs. The peace we all need and without which there is nothing. The peace Prince didn't have when he spilled his family's blood, and perhaps in another era, he would have been Rimbaud, Ulrich von Hutten, François Villon, but in this twenty-first century, he's nothing more than a fucking mental case.

I'll shut up now. I look at myself in the mirror and go silent. I've made a living from words, and now I hand them over, they are no longer mine, they belong to the air, they belong to the cathedral that will remain there in Cienfuegos when none of us are left—to *that*, my words belong to the Black Cathedral.

EMILIO SÁNCHEZ VÁZQUEZ, *director of Ariza prison*

We applied the protocol that by law and national guidelines is applied to every inmate who tests positive for HIV. This protocol includes a transfer to the prison's hospital, which is of course less strict than Ariza 2, the so-called Shark. He managed to escape from there. It's not anyone's fault since his case wasn't one of the worst. With good behavior, he would have been free in five years, more or less, so that escape was confusing for everyone. They say that *compañera* Sira Gómez, one of the shift nurses the night of the events, was involved. But what is certain is that during the investigation, nothing was proven, and this *compañera* was able to take up her work again without any problem. In the time that said David King Stuart Álvarez was imprisoned in Ariza 2, his behavior could be classified as dreadful. He had a brawl with a longtime inmate and caused several group fights because of his rebellious behavior. He was incapable of staying in line.

YUSIMÍ CABRERA

Cricket came to see me to say we should leave together, since Luisa, his Spanish girlfriend, was willing to get married and then a brother of hers was going to write me a letter of invitation so the three of us could arrive in Madrid together, and we would settle there, because the bars in Madrid are the best in the world, as Joaquín el Sabina says in so many songs.

"Are you crazy?" I said to him. "Antón has connections in Spain, if you didn't know; if you do this, you'll find out how powerful the Russian Mafia is in the world."

"Shit."

"I'm el Ruso's slave." I again showed him the scorpion that el Ruso had tattooed on all us girls so we wouldn't forget who we were, and I also told him that el Ruso had promised to poke out my eyes if I left him, and who's going to love a blind black girl?

"I'm going to love her. Besides, el Ruso can kiss my ass,

he's not anybody anymore. Look at how my father finished him off, if not for me, who went in his place, he'd be in the Shark now, living like Cain, because the one in charge there is Nacho Fat-Lips, and he could give a shit about el Ruso."

"Speaking of, what are you doing on the street? Did they give you parole?"

"I escaped."

I got up from the bed, and naked just like I was, I asked him to leave, I didn't want any more trouble than I already had. "I'm sorry," I said to him, "but don't come around here anymore . . . El Ruso found another big-cocked *mulato* and there's no sense in our continuing to see each other."

He looked at me from the bed with the disconcerted eyes of a child who has just had a toy taken away, and I felt bad for him, a little. I recognize that I was tough on him, but to survive in this concrete jungle, you've got to be made of steel, and I don't regret having treated him that way, especially when I later found out he had injected himself with HIV and had the nerve to come and see me, the real son of a bitch. He ruined my life because even though he wore a condom, some people think I have AIDS and give me dirty looks, and, well, I'm from Oriente and can't go back home just like that. Things are bad in Guantánamo, and even though I have some savings, I've spent a lot in taking care of these four walls that el Ruso finally allowed me to have.

When I told him to leave, he made as if to hit me, but held back in time. Even though he was big and all, if he laid a hand on me, I would have cracked his skull. Not even Antón hits me, and he took care of me when I got here and needed to get a leg up. So Cricket, when all he's ever done for me is screw me?

What we had was about pleasure, pure pleasure and business. Actually, people from Camagüey and people from Oriente don't have anything in common. During the Wars of Independence, there were more troubles between the troops of Carlos *el* Manuel de Céspedes and those of Ignacio *el* Agramonte than between the Spanish and the pro-independence *mambises*.

When he was leaving, he told me that if I didn't love him, he was going to put a rope around his neck.

"Do what you want, but remember that real men don't do that, and mothers suffer more than we do from that kind of madness."

"Give me my brother's book."

"No, you gave it to me." But then I started thinking, and it wouldn't have been good for me to have him make a scene, so I took the little book of poems and gave it to him, and I told him that, after all, they were selling it at the bookstore and I didn't need his gifts, and I went and grabbed all the dresses and watches he had given me and threw them at him, and he grabbed me and kissed me on the mouth by force, and I shouldn't have let him because that damn *maricón* had AIDS, but I didn't know it, although now I've come to the conclusion that HIV is like a cold, at the end of the day it's a virus and sometimes you get it and sometimes you don't. "I'm leaving," he said later, "see ya never," and he left through that door and never came back. What I know of him has been through the TV and through letters. Because when he was at the end, at the end because he refused to take medicines, he wrote me a goodbye letter, the most beautiful thing anyone has ever written me, I still keep it with me and read it only if I'm depressed, I mean, really depressed.

I didn't go to the burial, el Ruso didn't let me, he told me it wouldn't be appropriate. I would have liked to go so he wouldn't enter into death as alone as he had lived. I know what that's like, that at your burial there's not a single face of anyone who held you in the slightest consideration. They say that inside the casket, he was unrecognizable, skinny and battered like a mummy's skeleton. I feel so bad for him but life is like that, harsh like real vodka, not that shit they sometimes sell at the shopping center. I might go to Russia, el Ruso promised me that. *But Russia*, I said, *not Ukraine or anything like it*.

Antón *el* Abramovich, who still has a lot of dough even though the police shut down a lot of his businesses, said to me, "No problem, we won't stop until we get to Moscow, you're going to love the Kremlin and the white nights in Saint Petersburg."

"What about Margarita and your children?" I asked, because I'm not an asshole, I know how to respect the other woman.

"Of course they're coming with us," el Ruso said, "but before then, I'll adopt you so Margot doesn't blow up on me, and you'll be one more among my little black children; besides, you can't refuse me this, I want you to join the Orthodox Church."

Hot damn, I thought, *this girl from Guantánamo, becoming Orthodox and everything*.

GUTS

I wander around Las Ramblas slowly, as if I were carrying something fragile, and that fragile something is my own life.

Today there is all kinds of shouting, Real Madrid has fallen in an embarrassing way, and people from all over are coming out and beeping their horns and shouting, "Barcelona, Barcelona!" When Las Ramblas is like that, I feel like the loneliest man in the world. I get to my house and my wife hugs me, her skin is white like I always wanted, and when she laughs, she reveals all those teeth so white they seem fake, but they're real, and she has green eyes like Yusimí, the woman I never tried. Not because I was afraid of el Ruso, but because that black girl has a cloud over her head, and I wasn't going to let her ruin my life. Then in come Juan and Aitana, my children, the twins, and they also hug me and call me *negro*. In Barcelona, I like to be called that, as long as it's said with affection, not like in Cuba, where I was always defending myself as a *mulato*. I like finding myself here in Catalonia, so far away from all that, and when I get homesick, I go see Gaudí's cathedral and remember Cienfuegos, the neighborhood, and the Stuarts. I remember how those sons killed their own father. Yes, I remember, and sometimes, when I'm in the mood, I say, "Those *locos*!" And I limit myself to thinking of things like that, or sometimes I think that behind all that happened, there has to be an explanation we'll never understand because our brains can't process it. To kill your father and your mother to save your brother from AIDS, that's crazy. I always knew that Cricket hated old man Arturo, that he hadn't been able to forgive him for that time he almost died because of all the blows he took to the head when he caught him spying on that crazy Maribel, who must be a nasty old thing now. But, Jelly? No one ever did anything to him. He didn't get so much as a rose petal raised against him. He was always the beloved son.

The best dressed on the block. Gringo even left him his motor scooter when he took off. I don't understand it. The other day, here, in Barcelona, I saw Guido, the Italian guy who was Johannes's first husband, and I asked him. "I don't know," he said. He was wearing a checked shirt and a pair of shorts, riding a Harley-Davidson that yelled *rocker*, with some young chicks almost half his age. "Don't talk to me about Cuba and its black people, all of that is dead to me," he said to me, and I was about to punch him in the mouth, but I held back. That was around Diagonal, so I got back in my car and slammed down on the accelerator, getting as far away as possible from that Guido. Death has that way about it. It attracts you like the most perfect white woman, not one from Barcelona, but a British one. It attracts you and takes you wherever it wants, and when it has you there, it laughs. What happened to them was like what happened to me, who was going to take a guy out just on the basis of Gringo's advice. *You gotta kill an old kingpin, Guts, get yourself a reputation,* he said to me, and that was enough for me, I went to find the subject at his house and tried to get him to come out onto the street so I could knife him. That was enough for me. So I think that was enough for them, too. The morning, or afternoon, when Cricket went to see Prince to tell him he'd injected himself with AIDS and he was scared, and they both went to see Prince's Palo *Padrino* for advice, and he told them what they had to do: a ceremony that involved the blood of the oldest person to whom they were related; that morning, everything was written as if in stone, a type of indelible writing, and if I stop and think about it, I'm sure that the *Padrino* didn't think that they would really do it. He told them one of those things you say during a steamy

August when you want to rest and someone comes to interrupt you. *Do this*, the *Padrino* said in his tremendous, goddamned naïveté, thinking he was dealing with adults, after all, the two of them were easily taller than six foot two each, but they were children, wicked children like all of us, children without a childhood, the sons of trouble and evil.

IBRAHIM

Later everything clouded over. The temple was no longer good, everything clouded over. God didn't want it. God didn't want that temple, and everything started to get confusing. Good people died because God does not love human arrogance, the psalms say so, but if I start to cite them now, I'll never finish. Arturo Stuart died, and we disbanded like only the tribes of Israel can, and then we understood that we were a tribe, the lost tribe, and the cathedral was left alone, challenging the wind, serving as a gigantic nest for the birds. It was abandoned like a rocket ship that never took off, and the black Americans stopped donating money, and the Poder Popular stopped helping us with its building brigades, its trucks and cranes, and for a time only we remained, preventing the theft of stones, cement, sand, in case another sign from God arrived and told us to continue.

MARIO GARCÍA PUEBLA, *policeman*

It was about 6:05 in the morning. I had just gotten off my shift. I had had to take a captopril under my tongue because my blood pressure was sky-high. Irene, my wife, comes to me and says, *Mario, phone.* I went to the living room and picked up the receiver. Then I hear a voice that hits me with *Come over here, they've wiped out old man Stuart.* I thought it had been those people with that scabby blond vulture, el Ruso, Abramovich. But when I got to the station, they told me there was a witness. That witness was the wife of the deceased, Carmen Álvarez. She confirmed it was her own children, the sons. The daughter was studying in Havana. *Get over to Punta Gotica and process the crime scene,* the chief said to me, and I went to the alleyway where the deceased's neighbors and religious confreres were all wound up: they wanted to lynch anyone who struck them as suspicious. We were forced to call in for police backup to clear the place so we could focus on our job. At 10:00 a.m. we were able to process the crime scene.

The deceased was in the master bedroom, naked from the waist up. He had just one wound in his neck, caused by a sharp-edged weapon that seemed to have pierced his aorta. After a superficial examination, his body temperature and the blood deposits indicated that the death must have occurred between three and four in the morning. Finally, I told the photographer to take the obligatory photos and proceeded to lift the corpse.

The kids were found by the search brigade and captured close to the coast when they tried to hijack a boat to leave the country. They had $20,163 on them.

People wanted to hang them, so we had to request the army's cooperation to transfer them to the headquarters of the technical investigation department. From the beginning, they admitted their guilt.

ANIA MARTÍNEZ SAINZ, *National Revolutionary Police officer*

She was in a nervous state that is impossible to describe, and it's no wonder, she had witnessed her sons, the beings she'd brought out of her womb, killing their father and tying her up to kill her, too. I am a woman and a mother, besides being a police officer, and I wouldn't want to imagine anything similar happening to me. Classy, rather pretty despite her age, she couldn't speak coherently, even though she tried. She had to interrupt herself to cry and would then start over from the beginning. Her statement lasted almost two hours. She told us that at around two in the morning, Samuel Prince Stuart Álvarez, her younger son, had arrived with the other one, the inmate, David King Stuart Álvarez, and they looked high. Then they killed the father, Arturo Stuart, before he managed to try anything. Especially because he loved Prince very much and couldn't believe what he was hearing. "Did that one put this into your head?" was the only thing the deceased was able to ask before Prince jabbed the knife into his neck, shouting, "Die!"

They tied her up. She escaped because they had taken pills. Without a doubt, they had taken pills, and the knots weren't tight. She escaped while the two of them did satanic incantations around the old man's body to take away David King's AIDS.

"It's not their fault," the woman finally said. "They were possessed by demons."

Then she burst out crying and no one could make her continue her statement.

PABLO ARGÜELLES LARA, *the* Padrino

I didn't tell him to kill anyone, that's a lie. I didn't even know his brother had AIDS. I only told him how the dead would remove a wrong as bad as that, and I told him because he asked. I don't have anything to do with the murder. That girl, the writer, that Berta, she came here from Havana and offended me. She demanded the skull of an Aramís, *or else I'm going to the police*, she said. I don't have anyone's skull, but I can't go around taking things out of the Nganga, either, or else the *efumbe* will go through me and could even kill me. "I'm the *Padrino* to lots of people, not just Gringo or Prince, what fault is it of mine that these two turned out to be criminals? What fault is it of mine?" I said to her.

The one who was really to blame was the late Arturo Stuart, he wanted to mock nature and the gods, and his own God turned his back on him. I don't know why you're coming to see me. I just told Prince what I told the police, and that I would tell anyone who asks. *The formula to escape a terminal illness is to bring blood from your closest relative*, I would say, *the orishas created it in the darkness of time. Who am I to change that?* I said that and will say it again anytime I'm asked.

ARACELI

But what Berta will never know is that Prince and I were lovers, that I was with him at the same time that I was with her, that sometimes I would say I had to go somewhere, and it was so I could see Prince, together we went to the few cheap hotels in Cienfuegos, and sometimes the expensive ones because I still had some money, and he would steal from his father, he didn't tell me so, but I know he stole from his father, Berta will never know that, unless the dead man tells her, poor Aramís, who, after he died, never wanted to talk to me, as if I were to blame for everything, as if I had said to him: go to Cienfuegos and buy yourself a motorcycle, as if he had forgotten that the only thing I asked of my little *guajiro* who died so long ago was that he save me from Ferreiro, my husband, but that's life, it's exasperating. I haven't written anything else. When I left Cienfuegos I was burned out; besides, it's going well for me on television. You have a pretty face, people say, and I heard it so much that I ended up believing it, now I'm getting older and every day someone younger and prettier comes along. I wasn't born to be a lesbian. I'll never again face the circumstance of being another woman's wife. I was born to be with men, not even foreigners, I was born to be with Cuban men. Perhaps I'm a masochist and I like to be mistreated, but that's how it is. My current lover is a truck driver who comes to see me every time he comes back from Santiago, where he works, and he hits me, not hard, and not my face, but he does do it. I like that he hits me, but not hard. I like that no one at the TV station can stand my man and they ask me, *Araceli, how could someone like you, so classy, get together with a brute like him?* Then, when I feel like it, I tell them to go to hell, Cienfuegos-style. "Go fuck yourselves," I say to them, and then they understand that there's nothing classy about me, that I'm quite ordinary. I like for them to know so they're prepared. I like for no one to have any expectations of me. I'm nothing special, I tell them when they say that one of the last poems I wrote appeared in a given anthology. I didn't authorize it, I say, and it's because, in a fit of sexual fervor, I gave all my poems to Berta, and she's the one who publishes them in my name. *She's so crazy*, I think, because I haven't read any of her novels and don't plan to in the future. The only thing that mattered to me about her was her as a person, the same as Prince, his self. Although I knew he was bad, worse than a pig's bite, as they say in my town. He pissed on my face once, and it wasn't when we were fucking. I was sleeping and I felt a hot stream on my cheek, and it was Prince urinating on me as if I were a goddamn toilet. It was at the Jagua Hotel, in a room paid for by my money, I had just sucked him off to make him happy, something I don't like, ever since I was little, I've always hated to put things in my mouth, and despite this, to show me his great love, his esteem, he had to piss on my face. It's that he knew I was also Berta's lover, and that she loved my face, that's why he did it, to humiliate her. He was a bad guy, I'll repeat it, if not, he wouldn't have committed that horrible act when he had the whole world ahead of him. At that point, Prince was the god of poetry, I can say that because even though I don't write anymore, I read a lot. He didn't care about the future because he hated himself. It's a lie that he loved his brother so much, that madman who injected himself with AIDS in prison to go see a cheap whore like that Yusimí, and then when she rejected him, he didn't have the courage to face it, to say to himself, *I'm going to live HIV positive with all the dignity in the world*, and he went to see his brother to get him out of the bind, and what did they do? They tightened the screws: they killed their father and drenched their mother in blood to cure AIDS, isn't that just the lowest.

They have another car set aside for me, and when I sell this shitty Polish Fiat, I'll finish getting the money together to buy it. The money I have now has been given to me by several salsa and reggaeton bands so I can promote them on my program. It has taken me four years, but I have almost fifteen thousand dollars. Any day now I'll go to the car lot and acquire a Peugeot or an Audi, I don't want any of that Chinese shit that's flooded the market. I want an elegant, European car to rejuvenate me. When I buy it, I'll go see Berta, and if I'm in the mood, I'll let her kiss me, and if I'm still in the mood, I'll let her sleep with me and take out all of her novelist's frustrations on me. She has so many published books but never has enough money and still lives in that little apartment in La Víbora. I'm going to let her talk, but when I get tired of being her wailing wall, I'll tell her, *Don't you remember when you went to go see me with your cheap little shoes and your starving face and those bugged-out eyes that made you look crazy, to tell me about what a dead man wanted? Don't you remember? You always were low class*, I'll conclude, to see if she gets worked up and smacks me, it's been a long time since anybody hit me real hard. Even the truck driver is scared of me, since the last time I told him that if he hit me again, I would break his ass. Prince hit well. He hit like he meant it, and since he didn't like to be called Michael Jackson, I would shout, "Help! Michael is killing me!" And he would get furious. One day we went to a certain Edgar's home. He had a rented room in one of those apartments on the Boulevard in Cienfuegos, and after fucking, Prince fell asleep, so I took that notebook where he kept his poems and I burned it. "That's for pissing on my face," I told him when he woke up. He didn't say anything. He didn't explain that he had copies, but he stopped sleeping with me.

It was as if I'd turned invisible. He didn't see me, and to take revenge I started sleeping with Héctor, an Argentine medical student, and the one I ended up punishing was Berta, because it's what we all do, we initiate some action and nothing happens, everything is suspended in the air. My name is Araceli and I haven't gone to Cabaiguán in such a long time that I feel like I was born in Cienfuegos, the place where I arrived when I was seventeen years old already and married to a brute who oversaw a warehouse, and the lover of a young *guajiro*, who a big *mulato* they called Gringo killed just because, he hadn't done anything to him, a little *guajiro* who wanted to buy a motorcycle in Cienfuegos and ended up in the bellies of the residents of Punta Gorda, that exclusive neighborhood, where Berta and I went so few times, Prince and I went when we were lovers, and they would call her and me *bread with pasta* and call him and me *chocolate and vanilla*, because I've always been so pale. I would call him *heart of evil*.

I would say to him, "Prince, you're a heart of evil and you don't love anyone."

"It's true, I don't love anyone."

"Not even me?"

"Not even you."

"What about your mother and your father?"

"Not them, either."

"Your siblings?"

"Less still."

"What about poetry?"

"Poetry is some shit that with a little bit of luck will earn me a living."

"You think so? No one makes a living from that."

"I will," he would say.

When I was tired of playing, I would ask him seriously, so much so that the muscles of my face would flinch, "What about God, Prince, do you love God?"

He would usually get quiet, but one day he answered clearly, "God less than anyone else."

Was he already crazy? I don't know, I simply don't think so, but he had something of Achilles in him, he was fatalistic, and he knew he was going to get screwed like Gringo, his friend, his pal, and he wanted to get screwed big-time, in that pragmatic, mad way that he had. He was the most beautiful man I've slept with, although that's not saying much because I like ugly men. I like for women to be beautiful, like Berta when I met her at fourteen, with her svelte body and that curly *mulata*'s hair framing her face, or like Johannes, the famous painter coming to Cuba for the first time in twenty years to receive the National Culture Prize, what madness. Aren't we all mad? I'm sure they'll bring her to my show and give me orders like a dog, *Interview her, Araceli*, of course I'll do it, that's what they pay me for, and, well, I'll tell her one silly thing or other and then I'll ask her as I look into her light brown eyes, *Don't you remember me?* If she says no, I'll have the pleasure of saying, even if I get thrown off TV, *Well, I do, your family built a cathedral in Cienfuegos that's the maddest thing there ever was, and your brother, Prince, a poet and murderer by the looks of it, was my lover, I want you to know.* It doesn't matter to me if they shut down my show; after all, I have the money for my car, and I'll go see Berta, and we'll go off together, for a spin but nothing more, I'll repeat, I'll never again have the courage to accept myself as another woman's woman.

Then everything remained like an unfinished poem, like something that switches off and we can't prevent it, we can't, then everything remained. They're calling me and I go, they say, *Prince, come here,* and I do it. *Tell us what happened so we can laugh and then crow like a rooster and say that you killed your parents just so you could go to the party with all the orphans, say it, Prince, or we're going to set loose the night hounds to scare you, to ask you what happened to you, why you're so bad and so mad, tell it, but from the beginning, talk to us about your sister, Johannes, the one that's rich, and your brother, Cricket, the fucker who got AIDS, talk to us about when a madman like you decided to become a poet, tell us everything, young Prince, without leaving anything unsaid, or you'll see, you're mad, do you know? And if you don't, then figure it out, you killed your father. All of us want to kill our fathers at one time or another, but you did it, young Prince, that's why you're here until you die, and no one wants to have anything to do with you, no one, you're screwed, young Prince, you're screwed, who actually kills their mother or their father, which are one and the same thing? Your mother escaped because she untied the rope that you had her bound with, and all that to cure your brother's AIDS, it's not like you loved him that much. Did he get cured, by chance? No, he died in jail of AIDS, lucky for him, not like you, who will be here until the end and only go out that door once you're dead, to be buried in a goddamn tomb, a fucking nameless hole, and no one will remember you existed, young Prince, they'll forget you forever and at the hour of your death, mad fucking poet, who told you a black man had the right to be a poet? At the hour of your death, your*

God will be waiting for you, young Prince, the one in which you haven't stopped believing, to take revenge, because it's your fault that the cathedral was left unfinished, O young Prince! Hold out for a long while, cling to life strongly enough because so much awaits you, O young Prince! Fucking black madman, if you remember one of your poems, read it to us, and perhaps we'll give you an extra ration of bread, they say that your brother, the other black madman, had a terrifyingly large cock, is that true, young Prince? Let me see yours, let me at least touch it. If you let me, I'll lower your ration of pills, I promise you, let me.

It's not all bad, all of you are like that, well-endowed for naught, young Prince, for naught.

BERTA

One day the pigeons will take over the unfinished cathedral, they'll smother it with their wings, and when that day comes, I'm going to be in Cienfuegos to see it. Then time will pass, I will die, and with me everyone who lived in this time, but the photos will remain. Then the photos will die, along with anyone who can decipher a human face; later on, the heat will rise, and all of Cuba will end up underwater, and with Cuba, the cathedral; but later, when everything dries up and nothing remains, and the extraterrestrial voyagers find it, how will they know that this cathedral was never finished? They will think that it was once the main temple of a city of happy beings and that the parishioners' children once ran down its aisles, and over the course of time, will it matter that it wasn't like that?

A NOTE ABOUT THE AUTHOR

Marcial Gala was born in Havana in 1963. He is a novelist, a poet, and an architect, and is a member of UNEAC, the National Union of Writers and Artists of Cuba. He won the Pinos Nuevos Prize for best short story in 1999. *The Black Cathedral* received the Alejo Carpentier Prize for best novel and the Premio de la Crítica Literaria in 2012. He lives in Buenos Aires and Cienfuegos.

A NOTE ABOUT THE TRANSLATOR

Anna Kushner, the daughter of Cuban exiles, was born in Philadelphia and has been traveling to Cuba since 1999. She has translated the novels of Norberto Fuentes, Leonardo Padura, Guillermo Rosales, and Gonçalo M. Tavares, as well as two collections of nonfiction by Mario Vargas Llosa.